KINGFISHER TREASURIES

A *wealth of stories to share!*

Ideal for reading aloud with younger children, or for more experienced readers to enjoy independently, **Kingfisher Treasuries** offer a wonderful range of the very best writing for children. Carefully selected by an expert compiler, each collection reflects the real interests and enthusiasms of children. Stories by favorite classic and contemporary authors appear alongside traditional folk tales and fables in a lively mix of writing drawn from many cultures around the world.

Generously illustrated throughout, **Kingfisher Treasuries** guarantee hours of the highest quality entertainment and, by introducing them to new authors, encourage children to further develop their reading tastes.

KINGFISHER
Larousse Kingfisher Chambers Inc.
80 Maiden Lane
New York, New York 10038
www.lkcpub.com

First published in 1999
4 6 8 10 9 7 5
4TR / 0501 / THOM / (MA) / 115INDWF

LIBRARY OF CONGRESS CATALOGING-IN-PUBLICATION DATA
The Kingfisher treasury of pirate stories / chosen by Tony Bradman;
illustrated by Tony Ross.
p. cm.
Summary: A collection of stories about pirates and pirating,
by such authors as Joan Aiken, J. M. Barrie, and
Robert Louis Stevenson.
1. Pirates—Juvenile fiction. 2. Children's stories, English.
[1. Pirates—Fiction. 2. Short stories.] I. Bradman, Tony.
II. Ross, Tony, ill.
PZ5.T75525 1999
[Fic]—dc21   98-50248 CIP AC

ISBN: 0-7534-5190-5
Printed in India

THE
KINGFISHER TREASURY OF
Pirate Stories

CHOSEN BY TONY BRADMAN

ILLUSTRATED BY TONY ROSS

NEW YORK

CONTENTS

THE PIRATE SHIP

Ruth Ainsworth

The good ship *Sea Lion* was a fine sight with her sails spread like wings to catch every breeze. Whatever the weather, her flag flew at the masthead. It was the Jolly Roger, the pirate flag, with a skull and crossbones on it. Any ship that saw this fearful flag made off as fast as possible in the opposite direction.

The pirate chief was Captain Bones. He had ten sailors in his crew, all with black sea boots, and knives in their belts, and gold rings in their ears. They wore bright handkerchiefs tied around their heads, and they had frightening names like Pincher and Chopper and Scrag.

Life on board the *Sea Lion* was not very pleasant because there was no one to make the crew comfortable. They had to make their own beds and sew on their own buttons and do their own

washing. The food was dull, too, as it nearly all came out of tins. They had bully beef for dinner and supper on Sunday, Monday, Tuesday, Wednesday, Thursday, and Saturday. The day that was different was Friday. On Friday they had fish, which they caught fresh from the sea.

The pirates looked forward to Friday. They had the fun of catching the fish first and then the pleasure of eating it afterward. Sometimes the cook fried chips as well, and then there was not a jollier pirate crew afloat, eating their fish and chips, and passing the vinegar bottle from hand to hand.

One Friday morning the crew settled down as usual to catch their fish for dinner. Some trailed nets behind the ship. Some had rods and lines. Some lowered little wicker cages over the side to catch lobsters and crabs. Only the cook was in his galley, polishing his pots and pans, and slicing potatoes.

Time passed and no one had a single bite. The sun rose high and the deck became as hot as an oven, but still they had no luck. When it was almost dinnertime and the frying pans shone like mirrors, there was still nothing to put in them. Then Captain Bones himself came on deck, carrying his own favorite fishing net.

"I'll show you how to catch fish!" he roared. "Out of my way and I'll show you how to set to work!" He threw his net over the side and waited a few minutes, then began to haul it in. He hauled very slowly because it was so heavy.

"I've a good catch here," he said, "enough for today and tomorrow. It must be a shoal of herrings or else a huge cod. It might even be a whale. Why, my net's almost breaking! Lend a hand there! Look lively!" Pincher and Chopper hurried forward to help, and with a mighty heave they landed the net on deck.

"Shiver my timbers!" cried Captain Bones, when he saw what he had caught.

"Here's a pretty kettle of fish!" exclaimed Pincher.

Chopper said nothing, but stared and stared with round eyes.

There, tangled in the net, was a plump, shining mermaid, complete with long, scaly tail. She had golden hair and held a harp in her hand.

The cook came up from the galley with his kitchen knife in his hand.

"Now I can start dinner," he said, "and about time too!"

"But—but, you can't eat me," said the mermaid. "I am not a fish!"

"Begging your pardon, ma'am, you're half a fish. There are enough steaks in that tail of yours to give the crew a square meal and leave a nice bit over for fishcakes."

The mermaid began to cry, her golden hair hanging over her face like a curtain and her tears dripping on to the deck. Even Captain Bones felt sorry for her.

"Well," he said at last. "If we don't eat you, what are we to have for dinner? We can't have bully beef every day of the week. It's too much of a good thing."

The mermaid dried her eyes. "Let *me* cook your dinner today," she said. "Scrambled seagulls' eggs are very tasty."

"But we haven't any eggs—" began the cook.

"Never mind that. I'll see to the eggs."

The crew looked pleased at the thought of scrambled eggs, so the captain helped the mermaid out of the net and the cook took her down to his galley. She gave a shrill call through the porthole and a line of seagulls, one behind the other, flew into the galley in turn and laid a large egg in the biggest basin. A few minutes later, she and the cook were beating the eggs to a froth. Then they melted the butter and stirred up the scrambled eggs. The chips spat and sizzled, and when the bell went for dinner there was a piping hot meal on the table. The mermaid had even warmed the plates.

There was no talk of eating the mermaid after that. The captain gave her a cabin to herself, and in a few days she had settled down happily. She found some wool in a drawer and began to knit the captain a red pirate's cap with a tassel on top. When that was finished she started on stockings to wear inside his sea boots. Her tail came in most useful for winding the wool.

In the evening, just as the sun was setting, the mermaid always seemed to feel lonely. She sat on deck, gazing out to sea, and playing sad tunes on her harp. These sad tunes made the sailors think of their mothers, and they wished they had never left home and run away to be bold, bad pirates.

But once the sun had set and it was time to make the cocoa for bedtime, the mermaid cheered up, and the sailors cheered up, too. They sipped their cocoa and told stories and asked riddles and wondered whatever they did before they had a mermaid on board, a mermaid with yellow hair and a silvery fish's tail.

One day, Captain Bones told the crew that he was going to marry the mermaid. "You must call her Mrs. Bones in future," he ordered, "and do whatever she tells you."

The crew were upset by this news and they grumbled to each other as they did their work.

"Why should he have the mermaid all to himself?" complained Scrag. "She knits him caps and stockings, and I believe she has started on a jersey with yellow and black stripes."

"It isn't fair," agreed Pincher. "Have you seen the neat little shell buttons she has sewn on his shirt?"

"But we have to mend our own clothes," went on Chopper, "and do all the work of the ship!"

The next morning, when the captain went on his rounds to see that the crew was doing its duty, he was shocked to find that the deck had not been scrubbed. The brasses were not polished. The ropes were not tidily coiled.

"Look alive!" he roared. "This ship is a disgrace to any pirate. No work, no pay, you know."

Then Pincher, who was the bravest of the crew, came forward and made a speech:

"Captain Bones," he began, "we quite understand that this mermaid"—and here he bowed to Mrs. Bones—"belongs to you because you caught her in your net, but we each want a mermaid of our own. When Mrs. Bones plays her harp in the evening we feel lonely and sad.

Please find us some more mermaids to comfort us, and then we will do our work and the ship will be spick-and-span from bow to stern. We'll work from morning until night."

Captain Bones looked worried. "It was a piece of good luck," he said, "my catching a mermaid. You can hardly expect me to catch ten more."

"I think I may be able to help," said Mrs. Bones gently. "I have ten sisters who might care to leave their cave at the bottom of the sea and try life on board the *Sea Lion*."

"Oh, thank you, thank you!" cried the happy pirates.

"You must try hard to make them feel at home," went on Mrs. Bones. "The world under the water is very different from your world. It is cool and clean and quiet. My sisters are not used to loud voices or oily hands or rough ways."

The pirates promised to be very careful and they started straight away to prepare. They brushed their clothes and cut each other's hair and spring-cleaned the ship. Each made a present to give to his mermaid when she arrived. Pincher threaded a necklace of shells. Chopper carved a wooden spoon with a fish handle. Scrag made a dusting brush of seagulls' feathers. The others all thought of something suitable as well.

When all was ready, Mrs. Bones called softly, and from among the waves rose ten golden heads, and then ten white hands appeared, holding ten harps. The pirates let down rope ladders over the side of the ship and helped the mermaids to climb up onto the deck. Each mermaid was delighted with her present.

Life on board the *Sea Lion* was very different now that there were eleven ladies living there. The mermaids took it in turns to prepare the meals, and though their tastes were rather fishy, the men soon enjoyed their shrimp patties and lobster pies and seaweed salads. The deck was very crowded with mermaids

knitting for their husbands, mermaids combing their hair, and mermaids playing their harps. The pirates taught them to sing sea songs and the mermaids taught the pirates some of their own underwater music. These are some of the songs they liked singing. Of course they sounded much better with the harps twanging, and the pirates' deep voices booming, and the mermaids' shrill voices fluting the high notes.

Every evening at sunset the same strange sadness came over the new mermaids as had come over the first one. They sat gazing over the waves, twanging their harps, and sighing. Perhaps they wished they were little merbabies again, rocked in a cradle of coral with a pearl necklace around their necks, and a little oyster shell plate to eat off. But they soon cheered up.

The mermaids were very clean and tidy, and the ship was spotless. The only thing they did not like was the pirate flag, the Jolly Roger. "Such an ugly flag!" complained Mrs. Bones. "Such a horrid subject to choose! My sisters and I will make a prettier one."

They each sewed part of the new flag, and when it was finished there were eleven different pictures worked on it. Every picture was something to do with the sea—a shell or a fish or a piece of seaweed. The pirates admired it very much. But of course they were not really pirates now, with no pirate flag flying and with eleven beautiful mermaids on board. They were sailors instead, which was much safer and better.

Before long, they reached a desert island. They went on shore to explore. The sailors left the deep footprints of their boots in the sand while the mermaids' tails made winding tracks behind them. The island had a spring of fresh water for drinking and palm trees with monkeys and parrots in the branches. They decided to live there forever and ever and use the *Sea Lion* for fishing and for short trips around the coast.

The sailors built eleven palm-leaf huts and the mermaids set up housekeeping with half coconut shells for pudding basins. They lived happily ever after.

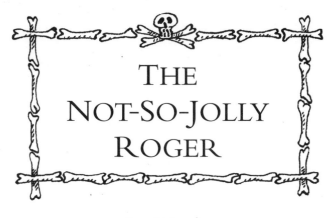

THE NOT-SO-JOLLY ROGER

Jon Scieszka

Joe, Fred, and Sam are three friends who make up the Time Warp Trio. With the help of The Book, a present given to Joe by his magician uncle, they can travel back and forth in time—although things never turn out quite as they hope! In this extract from one of their adventures, the boys encounter the legendary buccaneer Blackbeard, but find they have to teach HIM a trick or two to survive . . . .

"*Hickory dickory dock.
Mouse, turn back the clock.
The clock won't strike.
To where we like—*"

"Buried treasure," yelled Fred.

"No, you jerk," yelled Sam.

Fred threw his baseball. Sam ducked. Wisps of pale green mist began to swirl in my bedroom.

"But wait," I said, "the spell only works—"

Fred's baseball slowed and then froze in midair, only inches away from my desk lamp.

The Book seemed to melt right out of my hand.

The green mist swirled faster and higher; covering book, ball, bedroom, and all.

We looked around the island for somewhere to hide. The choices were pretty slim: our three trees, or one big black rock.

We climbed higher into our trees, and did our best to look like coconuts. We couldn't see anything, but we could hear the splash of oars and bits of some truly awful singing.

> *What do you do with a drunken pirate?*
> *What do you do with a drunken pirate?*
> *What do you do with a drunken pirate*
> *Ear-ly in the morning?*

The small rowboat landed as I peeked through the leaves. Two guys unloaded a chest. One was tall. The other was short. Both wore ragged pants and striped shirts. They were the ugliest and nastiest-looking guys I've ever seen . . . until I saw the third guy behind them. He was twice as big and twice as nasty-looking.

He was the one with the awful singing voice, and, boy, did he have a face to match. Black hair stuck out everywhere. His black eyebrows and mustache bristled out front. Long black strands fell down his back. And a monstrous black beard, with four pigtails, braided and tied with ribbons on the ends, fell down his chest. To top it all off—the whole mess was smoking!

But the worst part about this guy was not his crazy hair or black outfit. The worst part was that he was equipped, just as Sam had predicted, with four pistols and one wicked-looking cutlass.

"Bad luck," whispered Sam. "I'll bet anything that's Blackbeard . . . and not the Walt Disney version."

"Who's Blackbeard?" Fred whispered from his tree.

"His real name was Edward Teach," said Sam. "Some people say he was the craziest and meanest pirate of all time."

"Oh," said Fred.

The two ragged guys staggered up the beach lugging the chest between them. The giant black pirate counted off paces behind them.

"Eighteen, nineteen, twenty, twenty-one. *Halt!*"

They stopped right under our trees.

"Dig here, lads. We bury our treasure, and we three be the only ones what know about it, eh? Who says I don't treat me prisoners well? Have another tot o' rum."

The big guy pulled a bottle out of one of the deep pockets in his long coat. He took a swig, and passed it around.

The two prisoners drank, then started digging.

The pirate leaned against my tree. The top of his three-cornered hat was right below me. Something in his hair *was* fizzing and smoking, and it smelled terrible. I wiggled my nose as quietly as I could, and tried not to think about sneezing.

The pirate jabbed the sand with his cutlass. Then he started in with that singing again.

Come all you bold rascals what follow the sea,
To me way, hay, blow the man down,
Haul in yer sails and now listen to me,
And give me some time to ya de dee dee . . .

"Just us three, eh, laddies? Not a soul around."

Sam and Fred looked at me and bugged their eyes out.

The hot sun beat down. Flies buzzed around. The prisoners drank and dug. The bearded pirate kept singing—horribly. My foot, wedged behind a coconut, went to sleep. My arms felt like they were going next. Finally, after what seemed like hours, the two guys finished digging. The pirate slid his cutlass back in his belt.

"Yar, mates. That would be perfect. Now lower her in there slowly, slowly . . . ."

While the two prisoners were lowering the chest, the pirate pulled out two pistols and shot them both.

The bodies and chest fell to the bottom of the hole with an ugly thud. The crazy pirate laughed and started croaking another song as he kicked sand in the grave.

Sixteen men on a dead man's chest,
Yo, ho, ho and a bottle of rum.
Drink and the Devil will do the rest.
Yo, ho, ho and a bottle of rum.

A drop of sweat rolled off my nose and fell down toward the singing pirate. It landed right on his hat. I closed my eyes and held my breath.

He stood up, looked all around, and said, "Just us three, lads. Guard our secret well. Har, har, har." And then he turned to go.

That's when the fly decided to land on Fred's nose.

Fred wrinkled his nose, blinked, and shook his head.

The fly flew.

Fred's Mets cap slid right off his head, spinning down, down, down, until it landed with an awful *plop* right at the toe of the pirate's big, black boot.

He froze. He looked at the hat. Then he looked slowly up, up, up the trunk of my tree. Our eyes met and my heart went as numb as my foot. The black pirate growled, "*Arrrrrrrgh*," and grinned a crazy smile. I swear I saw his eyes flashing red.

Then he pulled out two pistols, aimed, and fired.

Click, went one pistol.

Click, went the other.

"Damnation and hellfire. Forgot to reload. But you won't be going nowhere, will you now, lad?"

My brain thought about diving out of the tree. My body refused.

The pirate tossed the two empty pistols aside and reached for two more.

While he was reaching, Fred slid down the trunk of his tree and jumped to the sand. "Don't shoot! That's my hat."

The pirate whirled around and aimed the pistols at Fred. "Yarrr, this island be haunted, sure. They're dropping from the trees. Quick, lad, how many more of your kind up there?"

"Two," said Fred.

"Three against one? Why, those are the best odds I've had in a long time." He tucked away one pistol and drew his cutlass. "Call out the rest of your spying monkeys. Let's fight to the death and the Devil take the hindmost."

Sam suddenly spoke up. "But we can't fight you." The pirate squinted up into the trees. "What's that? What do you mean you can't fight? Why in Hades not?"

"We can't fight you because . . . uhh . . . because we'd lose our Magician's License," said Sam.

"What?"

"Yeah, that's it," said Fred. "We're magicians— magicians from another time, and it's against Magic Rules for us to mess with anyone because we are so powerful."

"Magicians, eh?" The pirate itched his chin with the barrel of his pistol. "I'm a bit of a magician

myself. See that coconut? I'll make it disappear."
He fired his pistol. The coconut Fred had been
sitting behind exploded in a shower of milk and
shredded coconut.

The giant pirate laughed a scary, crazy laugh.
"Now get your magic selves down here where I
can see you."

Sam and I started down as fast as we could.

"Thanks, Sam," I said.

"And you best have some stronger magic than
that," he yelled, "or you'll be disappearing, too. Har,
har, har."

"Thanks a whole lot, Sam."

At ground level, the guy looked even bigger,
meaner, and uglier than from above. He did have
some smoking rope hanging in his hair. He did
have pigtails in his beard. And he did have crazy-
looking red eyes. The pirate slung his pistols and
looked the three of us over with those eyes. He
lifted Fred's hat from the sand on the tip of his
cutlass and jabbed it at him.

"So you three pips are magicians from another
time, are ye?"

He stared at Fred in his baseball uniform. Thin
wisps of smoke curled up around his three-
cornered hat. "And does everyone dress this funny
in your time?"

Fred pulled on his hat and muttered, "Look
who's talking."

"What was that, lad?"

"Oh, I said . . . enough talking."

"Right you are," said the pirate, towering over us. "So let's see some magic. Otherwise I might be thinking you were just spying on me and looking to steal a bit of me buried treasure." He smiled his nasty smile again. "And if I thought that, I'd have to kill you right now."

Fred gulped. "Uh . . . Eenie, meenie, mynie, mo. Catch a pirate by the toe. If he hollers, let him go. Eenie, meenie, mynie, mo!" Fred pointed to Sam. "Sam will now show you his powerful magic!"

The pirate wasn't smiling anymore.

Sam stepped forward on wobbly legs.

"Uh . . . hi, there, uh . . . Mr. Blackbeard," said Sam.

The pirate's dark face went suddenly white. "How do you know my name?"

"I read it," Sam said.

"Where's your crystal ball?"

"Oh, I don't need one. I even know your real name."

"Do you now?" Blackbeard looked around, then bent forward. "And what might it be?"

"Edward Teach."

Blackbeard staggered back a step and looked over his shoulder. "The Devil you say. You lads *are* magic."

My uncle Joe always says to work the crowd

when you've got them believing. I saw my chance
to impress Blackbeard even more with our
"magic."

"And what's that in your boot?" I said.

The big pirate looked down and jumped.
"What? What?"

I reached around his boot and held up a quarter.

Blackbeard snatched it out of my hand and gave
it a close look. "What strange doubloon is this?
That wasn't in my boot before."

Blackbeard stared at the quarter in his hand.

"You mean you lads can use your magic to pull
pieces of eight right out of the air?"

"Oh, sure," said Fred. "That's nothing for

powerful magicians like us. We could do that all day long."

"Could you now?" Blackbeard looked us over carefully.

We took a step back.

"I could use a few mates with your talents."

The three of us began to back away slowly.

Blackbeard slid his cutlass into his belt and put the quarter in his pocket. "Why don't you join me aboard my new ship?"

"Oh, we'd love to, but I have a . . . a . . . a big history report due Monday," said Sam.

"I call her the *Queen Anne's Revenge*." Blackbeard pulled another loaded pistol from his endless collection and pointed it between my eyes. "Do you think that's a nice name?"

I looked down the barrel of the biggest pistol I've ever seen.

"That's a very nice name," I said.

"Its previous owner ran into a bit of trouble . . . if you know what I mean."

Sam looked down the length of the cutlass. "I know what you mean."

"Would you like to join me on board then?"

Fred looked at Sam and me.

"We'd love to."

We marched down to the rowboat—the pirate ship anchored in the bay before us; Blackbeard, his loaded pistols, and his awful voice behind us.

Come all you bold pirates what follows the sea,
To me way, hay, blow the man down,
Just get me some magic and treasure for me,
And give me some time to blow the man down . . .

"Pirates didn't really make guys walk the plank, did they?" asked Fred.

"Nah, that's just in the movies," I answered, hoping it was true.

THE PIRATS

Colin McNaughton

Ladies and gentlemen, our hero: the incredible Anton B. Stanton, the smallest boy in the whole history of the world. He lived with his normal-sized mom, his normal-sized dad, and his normal-sized brothers in a normal-sized castle.

Being small was something Anton had grown used to. Indeed, being small had certain advantages: he often noticed things that other, bigger people would miss.

One hot and sticky summer afternoon, Anton was taking a cooling swim in the moat when he saw something very strange hidden among the reeds.

"Stone the crows!" said Anton. "It's a little ship!"

I wonder who this belongs to, thought Anton. Maybe I should take a look. He climbed aboard to explore. The ship seemed to be deserted. Suddenly he heard voices!

Too late to slip over the side, Anton found an empty barrel and clambered inside. As the voices came closer he looked up. At the top of the mast flew a rat skull and crossbones. Anton B. Stanton froze in horror. PIRATS!

"Trouble from the Water Rats!" bellowed the first Pirat. "You must be joking—weak as water, all of 'em!"

"Ha-ha, that's a good 'un!" laughed the second. "The princess won't even have time to squeak when we kidnap 'er!"

"Rat-nap! you mean, ha-ha!" joked the first. "Just think of the ransom! All that lovely gold an' silver! Ooh-arrgh!"

Anton shivered at the bottom of the barrel. And then it happened: he sneezed! Ah, AH, CHOO!

All at once, there were Pirats everywhere.

"It's a spy! Grab 'im! Give 'im a taste o' steel!" they shouted.

"No! Take 'im to the cap'n!" cried one. "'E'll know what to do with 'im!"

"We've captured a spy, Cap'n! Sneakin' about an' armed to the teeth!" lied one of the crew proudly.

"Well, well, well," growled Captain Ratfink, in a horrible rattle. "So, the Water Rats is sendin' little 'uman spies now, eh? Well, blast yer breeches! I'll teach you an' yer lily-livered masters a lesson y'll never fergit! Prepare the plank, me lads! Let's 'ave some fun afore we kidnaps the princess. Ooh-arrgh!"

The Pirats sailed the bad ship *Rattlesnake* into the deepest part of the moat.

"You won't get away with this!" cried Anton.

"Ha-ha!" laughed Ratfink. "That's what you think! Yer doomed, me lad, doomed! Y'hear? Ooh-arrgh! Ha-ha! Now jump! Or y'll feel me steel! Ha-ha!"

The crew cheered as Anton toppled from the plank, hit the water, and began slowly to sink. Down, down, down, he went. Down into the deep blue silence . . . .

Anton struggled to free himself but it was useless. Thoughts rushed through his head: Mom and Dad will never know what happened to me . . . . They'll . . . Oh!

Suddenly, out of the blue, he saw two shapes swimming towards him. Water Rats!

They grabbed Anton and swam for the shore as fast as their paws could take them. They pulled the coughing, spluttering Anton ashore.

"You saved my life," panted Anton. "Just wait till I get my hands on that Ratfink! But listen, perhaps I can pay you back for your kindness. You must take me to your king. I must speak to him at once!"

In the palace of the Water Rats, Anton told his story to the astonished court.

"Oh dear!" cried the King. "Oh dear! Oh dear, dear, dear! How terrible, how horrible, how, how NASTY! We must lock the doors and hide the princess. Send for the Princess Lily, Prime Minister."

"But, Sire," replied the PM, "she's out taking her afternoon walk by the . . . moat!"

The King turned pale. The Queen fainted. The throne room was silent.

Suddenly, the Royal Nurse burst into the room screaming, "The princess is kidnapped! The princess is kidnapped!"

"We must save her!" cried Anton. "Let's get after them."

"Er, well, yes, I, um, we, that is," dithered the King, digging furiously in his robes. "Now, where did I put the key to the armory? Must sharpen the swords. Er, um, Prime Minister, we do have swords, don't we?"

"Er, well, I, er, that is I'll have to check the records, Your Majesty," said the Prime Minister, his knees knocking like castanets.

"Hurry up!" shouted Anton. "They'll get away!"

But no one moved.

"We must attack at once with every Water Rat you have!" shrieked Anton.

"Er, well, you see, er, armies take time," said the King. "Er, um, Pirats, you say . . . ."

"Will no one come with me?" demanded Anton.

The courtiers shuffled their feet and avoided his eyes.

"I'll come," said a little rat called Twitcher.

"Good for you!" said Anton. "Get me some dry clothes and a sword and we'll go on ahead."

"Jolly good idea," muttered the King.

"Go on ahead and we'll er, um . . . ."

But Anton and Twitcher had gone.

"Ha-ha!" laughed Ratfink. "That were the easiest day's work I've ever done!"

"Let me go," screamed the Princess Lily. "Just wait till my father hears about this!"

"Your father," cackled Ratfink, enjoying himself, "is as soft as clarts! As weak as water! He's a drip! He couldn't punch his way out of a wet paper bag! Ya-ha!"

The other two Pirats were helpless with laughter at their captain's jokes.

"Let me at 'em!" hissed Twitcher.

"No!" said Anton, holding him back. "We'll have

to wait till dark. Maybe by then some of your Water Rats will have joined us."

Darkness came, but the reinforcements did not.

"Looks like it's up to us," said Anton. "Come on, let's go."

Silently they climbed the mooring ropes of the *Rattlesnake*. They found the princess, tied to the mainmast and fast asleep. (Ratfink, never dreaming the Water Rats would attempt anything so brave as a rescue, had not even bothered to post a guard.)

"This is going to be easy!" whispered Anton to Twitcher.

Anton slashed through the ropes.

Princess Lily woke with a start and, thinking it was the Pirats, screamed, "Take your hands off me, you smelly sewer rats! You vermin!"

Before Anton could explain, the ship was alive with startled Pirats.

"Quick, Twitcher!" cried Anton. "Get the princess out of here, I'll hold them for as long as I can!"

"It be a ghost!" yelled the Pirats.

"Ghost or not," bellowed the captain, "'e's no match for Ratfink the Pirat! Let's get 'im!"

And the fight began. The crew cheered as slowly but surely Anton, fighting furiously, was forced back and back, until at last he could retreat no farther.

"Shiver me whiskers!" laughed Ratfink. "This 'ere's no ghost; 'e fights like a rat! Ooh-arrgh!"

But Anton knew it would soon be over.

The end was near.

Suddenly from behind the Pirats came a mighty cheer. It came from a hundred furious Water Rats swarming aboard the *Rattlesnake*, screaming and yelling and waving their swords in the air.

Ratfink quickly recovered from his shock. "Avast, me 'earties," he cried to his crew. "Ha-ha! They're only Water Rats lettin' off a bit o' steam! They're no match for Pirat steel."

But his crew weren't listening. They were running for their lives. Running and jumping over the side like, well, like rats deserting a sinking ship!

Ratfink fought bravely, but he was outnumbered a hundred to one.

The clashing and flashing of steel filled the moonlit night. At last Ratfink lost his footing and fell with a yell into the moat.

The crew dragged their captain into the ship's rowing boat and the *Rattlesnake* Pirats lurched off into the night, to the sound of Water Rat cheers and the rasping voice of Ratfink cursing horribly.

The King of the Water Rats thanked Anton, then the Princess Lily kissed him. Anton blushed down to his toes.

"Er, well, er, I, er had better be going," said Anton. "My family will be ever so worried about me."

To the thunderous applause of the Water Rats,

Anton said farewell to Twitcher and slid down the mooring ropes to the bank.

The warm lights of the castle welcomed our hero home.

As he walked across the drawbridge, Anton B. Stanton shouted into the night, "Shiver me timbers, but fightin' pirats makes a fellow hungry. Ooh-arrgh!"

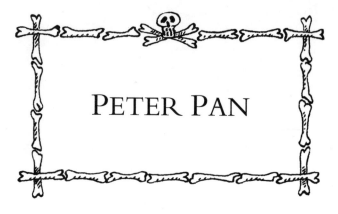

PETER PAN

J.M. Barrie
An extract retold by Joan Collins

Peter Pan, the boy who never grew up, takes Wendy, Michael, and John to Neverland, where they meet the Lost Boys, who call Wendy "Mother." But Peter has a deadly enemy, Captain Hook, whose hand he once chopped off in a fight. He tossed it to a crocodile who liked the taste so much he has followed Hook ever since, hoping to eat the rest of him. Hook has always been able to escape because the crocodile also swallowed a clock, and the ticking from inside has given him away. In this extract, the rivalry between Peter and Hook reaches its climax . . . .

At ten o'clock that night, Peter was awakened by a tiny knock on the door. It was Tinker Bell, who told him that Wendy and the boys had been captured and taken to the Pirate ship.

"I'll rescue them!" cried Peter, grabbing his sword. "But first I must take my medicine!"

"No! No!" cried Tinker Bell. "It's poisoned!"

"How could it be?" said Peter. "Nobody has been down here." He put the glass to his lips. But

 brave Tinker Bell had heard Hook talking to himself in the wood, and flew between Peter's mouth and the glass. She drank the poison herself, in one gulp.

"It *was* poisoned!" she cried. "I shall die!"

She fluttered feebly to her tiny couch and lay there gasping. Her light was getting weaker every moment. Soon it would go out.

Tink was whispering something. Peter bent down to listen. "If enough children believe in fairies," she gasped, "I might get better again!"

What could Peter do? Children everywhere were asleep. Then he thought of those who were dreaming of Neverland. He called, "If you believe in fairies, *clap your hands*! Don't let Tink die!"

There was silence. Then there was a faint sound of clapping. It grew and grew until it filled the cave. Tink was saved! Her voice grew strong and she flashed around the room, as merry as ever.

"And now to rescue Wendy!" cried Peter.

He came up through the tree into the moonlit wood. No one was about, except for the Crocodile, who never slept, passing down below.

Peter swore a terrible oath: "It's Hook or me this time!"

46

Aboard the *Jolly Roger*, Hook had the boys dragged up from the hold. He promised to spare two of them if they would join the crew.

"Would we be free subjects of the King?" asked John, bravely.

"You would have to swear 'Down with the King!'" growled Hook.

"Then we say *No!*" was the answer.

"Bring out the plank!" roared Hook. "And fetch their mother!"

Wendy was brought up to see her boys walk to their death in the briny ocean.

"Have you any last message for your children?" sneered Hook.

Wendy spoke out firmly: "All your mothers hope you will die bravely like true Englishmen!"

"Tie her to the mast!" Hook screamed.

The boys' eyes were on the plank. It was the last walk they would ever take. There was a grim silence—but it was broken by a strange sound: the *tick, tick, tick* of the Crocodile!

Hook collapsed with fear. He crawled along the deck, crying to his men, "Hide me! Hide me!"

As the crew gathered around Hook, the boys looked over the side and saw—not the Crocodile, but Peter Pan! *He* was ticking! Signaling to the boys not to give him away, he slipped aboard and ran to hide in the Captain's cabin.

When the ticking stopped, Hook grew brave again. He lined up the boys for a flogging and sent Jukes to his cabin for the cat-o'-nine-tails.

Jukes entered the dark room. Suddenly there was a terrible scream; a bloodchilling crow followed. Jukes had been killed by Peter!

Two more Pirates suffered the same fate.

After this the crew lost its nerve, and no one else would venture forth. So Hook sent in the eight boys. "Let them kill each other!" he snarled.

This was just what Peter wanted. He unlocked the boys' chains with a key he had found, and armed them with Hook's weapons. Then, while the Pirates' backs were turned, they all crept out on deck. Peter freed Wendy and, wrapping himself in her cloak, took her place at the mast. Then he let out a terrific *"Cockadoodle-doo!"*

The Pirates, frightened out of their wits, spun around. "'Tis an unlucky ship," they cried, "that has a captain with a hook!"

"'Tis because we have a woman on board," said Hook quickly. "Fling her over the side!"

"No one can save you now, missy!" said one of the kinder Pirates sadly.

"Here's one who can!" cried Peter, throwing aside the cloak. "Peter Pan!"

A great fight began. Swords and cutlasses clashed, and bodies tumbled into the water. Soon only Hook was left. His sword flashed like a circle of fire.

"Leave him to me, boys!" cried Peter.

Although he was smaller, Peter was nimbler and soon wounded Hook. At the sight of his own blood, Hook turned pale and dropped his sword. He rushed to set fire to the powder magazine and blow the ship up. But Peter bravely snatched the torch from his hand and threw it into the sea.

Hook backed away from the menacing Peter and climbed on the bulwark. Peter aimed a kick at him, and Hook lost his balance, slithering straight down into the sea.

The Crocodile, whose clock had run down at last, had silently followed Peter and was waiting patiently below. As Hook reached the water, the Crocodile opened his jaws—and finally had the rest of Hook for his supper.

That night the boys slept in the Pirates' bunks, and next morning they set off for home, with Peter as captain.

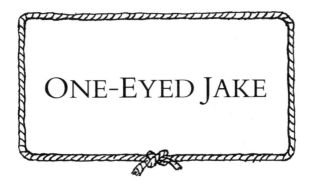

ONE-EYED JAKE

Pat Hutchins

Once there was a pirate called One-Eyed Jake. He had a horrible face, a terrible voice, and an awful temper.

Nobody liked him. The cook was terrified of him, the boatswain was frightened of him, and Jim the cabin boy was scared of him.

One-Eyed Jake robbed every ship in sight. He robbed the enormous passenger ships of their treasures, and dropped them into the hold.

He robbed the huge cargo boats of their cargo, and tossed that into the hold.

He even robbed the little fishing boats of their catch and shoved that into the hold, too. And if anyone dared complain, he threw him overboard.

One day the cook said, "I'm tired of stealing for One-Eyed Jake. I'd like to cook nice dinners on an enormous passenger ship."

And the boatswain said, "I'm tired of stealing, too. I'd like to steer a big cargo boat."

And Jim the cabin boy said, "I don't like stealing, either. I'd like to work on a little fishing boat and take the cat with me."

But they didn't dare complain to One-Eyed Jake, in case he threw them overboard. So they kept robbing and plundering until the ship's hold was so full that they had to pile the loot on the deck. But still One-Eyed Jake wanted more.

He spotted an enormous passenger ship, and robbed the passengers of their jewelry, but the hold was so full, and the loot so heavy, that the boat started sinking.

"Ha-ha!" said the passengers. "Your ship will sink with the weight of the jewels!"

"Ha-ha, yourself!" said One-Eyed Jake, and knowing that the cook was heavier than the jewels, he tossed him on to the passenger ship, and sailed away.

Then he spied a big cargo boat, and robbed the crew of their cargo of peacock feathers, but the hold was so full, and the loot so heavy, that the boat started sinking.

"Ho-ho!" said the crew. "Your ship will sink with the weight of the feathers!"

"Ho-ho, yourself!" said One-Eyed Jake, and knowing that the boatswain was heavier than the feathers, he threw him on to the cargo boat, and sailed away.

Then he saw a little fishing boat, and robbed the fishermen of their catch, but the hold was so full, and the loot so heavy, that the boat started sinking.

"Hee-hee!" said the fishermen. "Your ship will sink with the weight of the fish!"

"Hee-hee, yourself!" said One-Eyed Jake, and knowing that Jim the cabin boy was heavier than the fish, he threw him on to the fishing boat.

But Jim, who was a clever lad, shouted, "Here's the key to the cabin!"

And One-Eyed Jake, who was not so clever, caught it in his hand.

But the hold was so full, and the loot so heavy, that before anyone could say,

"Ha-ha! Ho-ho! Hee-hee! Your ship will sink with the weight of the key!"

. . . it had.

The cook was very happy cooking nice dinners on the enormous ship, the boatswain was very happy steering the huge cargo boat, and Jim the cabin boy was very happy working on the little fishing boat with the cat.

And One-Eyed Jake was never seen again.

THE
PARROT PIRATE
PRINCESS

Joan Aiken

The King and Queen were quarreling fiercely over what the baby Princess was to be called when the fairy Grisel dropped in. Grisel, that is to say, did not drop in—to be more accurate, she popped out of one of the vases on the mantelpiece, looked around, saw the baby, and said:

"What's this?"

"Oh, good afternoon," said the King uncomfortably.

"We were just putting you on the list of people to be invited to the christening," said the Queen, hastily doing so. She had presence of mind.

"Mmmmm," said Grisel. "Is it a boy or a girl?"

"It's a girl, and the sweetest little—"

"*I'm* the best judge of that," interrupted the fairy, and she hooked the baby out of its satin cradle. "Well, let's have a look at you."

The baby was a calm creature, and did not, as the Queen had dreaded, burst into loud shrieks at the sight of Grisel's wizened old face. She merely cooed.

"Well, you can't say she's very handsome, can you? Takes too much after both of you," Grisel said cheerfully. The baby laughed. "What are you going to call her?"

"We were just wondering when you came in," the Queen said despairingly. She knew that Grisel had a fondness for suggesting impossible names, and then being extremely angry if the suggestions were not taken. Worse, she might want the baby called after herself.

"Then I'll tell you what," said Grisel, eagerly leaning forward. "Call it—"

But here she was interrupted, for the baby, which she still held, hit her a fearful whack on the front teeth with its heavy silver rattle.

There was a terrible scene. The King and Queen were far too well-bred to laugh, but they looked as if they would have liked to. The Queen snatched the baby from Grisel, who was stamping up and down the room, pale with rage, and using the most unladylike language.

"That's right, laugh when I've had the best part of my teeth knocked down my throat," she snarled. "And as for you, you—" She turned to the baby, who was chuckling in the Queen's arms.

"Goo goo," the baby replied affably.

"Goo goo, indeed. I'll teach you to repeat what I say," the fairy said furiously. And before the horrified Queen could make a move, the baby had turned into a large, gray parrot and flown out of the window.

Grisel smiled maliciously around the room and said: "You can take me off the christening list now."

She went, leaving the King and Queen silent.

The parrot turned naturally to the south, hunting for an island with palm trees, or at least a couple of coconuts to eat. After some time she came to the sea. She was disconcerted. She did not feel that she could face flying all the way over that cold gray-looking water to find an island that would suit her. So she sat down on the edge to think. The edge where she sat happened to be a quay, and presently a sailor came along, said, "Hello, a parrot," and picked her up.

She did not struggle. She looked up at him and said in a hoarse, rasping voice: "Hello, a parrot."

The sailor was delighted. He took her on board his ship, which sailed that evening for the South Seas.

This was no ordinary ship. It was owned by the most terrible pirate then in business, who frightened all the ships off the seas. And so fairly soon the parrot saw some surprising things.

The pirates were quite kind to her. They called her Jake, and took a lot of interest in her education. She was a quick learner, and before the end of the voyage she knew the most shocking collection of swear words and nautical phrases that ever parrot spoke. She also knew all about walking the plank and the effects of rum. When the pirates had captured a particularly fine ship, they would all drink gallons of rum and make her drink it too, whereupon the undignified old fowl would lurch about all over the deck and in the rigging, singing,

"Fifteen men on a dead man's chest, Yo, ho, ho, and a bottle of rum," and the pirates would shout with laughter.

One day they arrived at the island where they kept their treasure, and it was all unloaded and rowed ashore. It took them two days to bury it, and the parrot sat by, thinking: "Shiver my timbers, but I'd like to get away and live on this island!" But she could not, for one of the pirates had thoughtfully tied her by the ankle to a tree. She sat swearing under her breath and trying to gnaw through the rope, but it was too thick.

Luck, however, was with her. The second day after they had left the island, a great storm sprang up, and the pirates' ship was wrecked.

"Brimstone and botheration and mercy me!" chorused the pirates, clinging frantically to the

rigging. They had little time for more, because with a frightful roar the ship went to the bottom, leaving Jake bobbing about on the waves like a cork.

"Swelp me," she remarked, rose up and flew with the wind, which took her straight back to the island.

"Well, blow me down," she said when she got there. "This is a bit better than living on biscuits among all those unrefined characters. Bananas and mangoes, bless my old soul! This is the life for me."

She lived on the island for some time, and became very friendly with a handsome gray gentleman parrot already there, called Bill. Bill seemed to know as much about pirates as she did, but he was always rather silent about his past life, so she gathered that he did not want it mentioned. They got on extremely well, however, and lived on the island for about twenty years, which did not change them in the least, as parrots are notoriously long-lived.

Then one day, as they were sharing a bunch of bananas, a frightful hurricane suddenly arose, and blew them, still clutching the bananas, out to sea.

"Hold on tight!" shrieked Bill in her ear.

"I am holding on," she squawked back. "Lumme, Bill, you do look a sight. Just like a pincushion!"

The wretched Bill was being fluffed out by the wind until his tail feathers stood straight up. "Well, you're not so pretty yourself," he said indignantly, screwing his head around to look at her. "Don't half look silly, going along backward like that."

"Can't you see, you perishing son of a sea-cook," squawked Jake, "it stops the wind blowing your feathers out—have a try."

"It makes me feel funny," complained Bill, and he went back to his former position, still keeping a tight hold on the bananas.

"Mountains ahead—look out!" he howled, a moment or two later. They were being swept down at a terrific speed toward a range of hills.

"Is it the mainland?" asked Jake, swiveling around to get a glimpse. "Doesn't the wind make you giddy?"

"Yes. It's the mainland, I reckon," said Bill. "There's houses down there. Oh, splice my mainbrace, we're going to crash into them. Keep behind the bananas." Using the great bunch as a screen, they hurtled downward.

"Mind last week's washing," screamed Jake, as they went through a low belt of gray cloud. "I never in all my life saw anything to beat this. Talk about seeing the world." They were only twenty feet above ground now, still skimming along, getting lower all the time.

"Strikes me we'd better sit on the bananas if we don't want our tail feathers rubbed off," said Jake. "Oh my, look where we're going."

Before Bill had time to answer, they went smack through an immense glass window, shot across a room, breaking three vases on the way, and came to rest on a mantelpiece, still mixed up with the bananas, which were rather squashed and full of broken glass.

"Journey's end," said Jake. "How are you, Bill?"

"Not so bad," said Bill, wriggling free of the bananas and beginning to put his feathers to rights.

Then they were both suddenly aware of the fairy Grisel, sitting in one corner of the room, where she had been knocked by a vase, and glaring at them. She picked herself up and came and looked at them closely.

"It's you again, is it?" she said. "I might have known it."

"Pleased to meet you," said Jake, who had no recollection of her. "I'm Jake, and this is my husband Bill."

"I know you, don't you worry," said Grisel. Then Jake suddenly remembered where she had seen Grisel before.

"Oh lor, don't you go changing me into a princess again," she cried in alarm, but hardly were the words out of her beak when, bang, she was back in her father's palace, in the throne room. She looked down at herself, and saw that she was human once more.

"Well! Here's a rum do," she said aloud. "Who'd have thought it?" She glanced around the room and saw, through a french window, the King and Queen, a good deal older, having tea on the terrace. There was also a girl, not unlike herself. She went forward to them with a very nautical gait, and hitching up her trousers, only it was a long and flowing cloth-of-gold skirt.

"Hello, Pa! Pleased to meet you!" she cried, slapping the King on the back. "Shiver my timbers, Ma, it's a long time since we met. Not since I was no longer than a marlin spike. Who's this?"

They were all too dumbfounded to speak. "Hasn't anyone got a tongue in their head?" she asked. "Here comes the prodigal daughter, and all they can do is sit and gawp!"

"Are you—are you that baby?" the Queen asked

faintly. "The one that got taken away?"

"That's me!" Jake told her cheerfully. "Twenty years a parrot, and just when I'm beginning to enjoy life, back I comes to the bosom of my family. Shunt my backstay, it's a funny life."

She sighed.

The King and Queen looked at one another in growing horror.

"And this'll be my little sissy, if I'm not mistaken," said Jake meditatively. "Quite a big girl, aren't you, ducks? If you'll excuse me, folks, I'm a bit thirsty. Haven't had a drink for forty-eight hours."

She rolled indoors again.

"Well, I suppose it might be worse," said the Queen doubtfully, in the horrified silence. "We can *train* her, can't we? I suppose she'll have to be the heir?"

"I'm afraid so," said the King. "I hope she'll take her position seriously."

"And what happens to *me?*" demanded the younger sister shrilly.

The King sighed.

During the next two months the royal family had an uncomfortable time. Jake obviously meant well, and was kindly disposed to everyone, but she did make a bad Crown Princess. Her language was dreadful, and she never seemed to remember not to say "Stap my vitals" or something equally unsuitable, when she trod on her skirt. She said that trains were a nuisance.

"You don't want to traipse around with the drawing room curtains *and* the dining room tablecloth pinned to your tail. I'm used to flying. Splice my mainbrace!" she would cry.

She rushed about and was apt to clap important court officials and ambassadors on the back and cry, "Hello! How's the missus, you old son of a gun?" Or if they annoyed her, she loosed such a flood of epithets on them ("You lily-livered, cross-eyed, flop-eared son of a sea-cook") that the whole Court fled in horror, stopping their ears. She distressed the King and Queen by climbing trees, or sitting rocking backward and forward for hours at a time, murmuring, "Pretty Poll. Pretty Jake. Pieces of eight, pieces of eight, pieces of eight."

"Will she *ever* turn into a presentable Queen?" said the King despairingly, and the Queen stared hopelessly out of the window.

"Perhaps she'll marry and settle down," she suggested, and so they advertised for princes in the *Monarchy's Marriage Mart*, a very respectable paper.

"We'll have to think of Miranda, too," the King said. "After all, she was brought up to expect to be Queen. It's only fair that she should marry some eligible young Prince and come into a kingdom that way. She's a good girl."

Eventually a Prince arrived. He came quite quietly, riding on a fiery black horse, and stayed at an inn near the Palace. He sent the King a note, saying that he would be only too grateful for a sight of the Princess, whenever it was convenient.

"Now, we must really try and make her behave presentably for once," said the Queen, but there was not much hope in her voice.

A grand ball was arranged, and the Court dressmakers spent an entire week fitting Jake to a white satin dress, and Miranda obligingly spent a whole evening picking roses in the garden to put in Jake's suspiciously scarlet hair.

Finally the evening came. The throne room was a blaze of candlelight. The King and Queen sat on the two thrones, and below them on the steps, uncomfortably but gracefully posed, were the two Princesses. A trumpet blew, and the Prince entered. The crowd stood back, and he walked forward and bowed very low before the thrones. Then he kissed Miranda's hand and said:

"Will you dance with me, Princess?"

"Hey, young man," interrupted the King, "you've made a mistake. It's the other one who's the Crown Princess."

Jake roared with laughter, but the Prince had gone very pale, and Miranda was scarlet.

"I didn't know *you* were the Prince of Sitania," she said.

"*Aren't* you the Princess, then?" he said.

"Have you two met before?" the King demanded.

"Last night in the Palace gardens," said Miranda.

"The Prince promised he'd dance the first dance with me. But I didn't know, truly I didn't, that he was *that* Prince."

"And I thought you were the Crown Princess," he said. There was an uncomfortable silence. Jake turned away and began humming *"Yo, ho, ho, and a bottle of rum."*

"Your Majesty, I am sorry to be so inconvenient," said the Prince desperately, "but may I marry *this* Princess?"

"How large is your kingdom?" asked the King sharply.

"Well, er, actually I am the youngest of five sons, so I have no kingdom," the Prince told him, "but my income is pretty large."

The King shook his head. "Won't do, Miranda must have a kingdom. I'm afraid, young man, that it's impossible. If you wanted to marry the other Princess and help reign over this kingdom, that would be different."

The Prince hung his head, and Miranda bit her lip. Jake tried to put her hands in her white satin pockets, and whistled. The crowd began to shuffle, and to quiet them the Royal Band struck up. And then Jake gave a shriek of delight, and fairly skated across the marble floor.

"*Bill,* my old hero! I'd know you anywhere!" A burly pirate with a hooked nose and scarlet hair was standing in the doorway.

"Well, well, well!" he roared. "Looks like I've bumped into a party. You and I, ducks, will show them how the hornpipe ought to be danced." And solemnly before the frozen Court they broke into a hornpipe, slow at first, and then faster and faster. Finally they stopped, panting.

"I'm all of a lather. Haven't got a wipe, have you, Jake?" Bill asked.

"Here, have half the tablecloth." She tore a generous half from her twelve-foot train and gave it to him. They both mopped their brows vigorously. Then Jake took Bill across to where the King and

Queen were standing with horror-struck faces.

"Here's my husband," said Jake. The Court turned as one man and fled, leaving the vast room empty but for the King and Queen, Jake and Bill, and Miranda and the Prince.

"Your husband? But you never said anything about him. And here we were, searching for princes," the Queen began.

"I don't think you ever asked me for my news," said Jake. "And now, if you'll excuse us, we'll be going. I've waited these two months for Bill, and a dratted long time he took to get here. Told him my address when we were parrots together, before all this happened, and a nasty time I've had, wondering if he'd forgotten it. But I needn't have worried. Slow but sure is old Bill," she patted his shoulder, "aren't you, ducks?"

"But—" said the Queen.

"Think I really stayed here all this time learning how to be a lady?" Jake said contemptuously. "I was waiting for Bill. Now we'll be off."

"But—" began the King.

"Don't be crazy," said Jake irritably. "You don't think I could stop and be queen *now*—when all the Court have seen me and Bill dancing like a couple of young grasshoppers? You can have those brats—" she nodded towards Miranda and the Prince, who were suddenly looking hopeful. "Well, so long, folks." She took Bill's hand and they went out.

And now, if you want to know where they are, all you have to do is go to the island where they lived before, and directly over the spot where the treasure was hidden, you will see a neat little pub with a large signboard: "The Pirate's Rest," and underneath: *"By Appointment to Their Majesties."*

SKULDUGGERY

Tony Robinson

I stood on the threshold of my new school, heartily proud of my uniform. A red spotted handkerchief was tied jauntily around my head, my moleskin sea boots were spick-and-span, as was my buckled belt and golden earring, and my blue-and-white-striped shirt had not a single bloodstain on it. "Squire Trelawney's Academy for Young Sea Dogs" announced the creaky sign above my head. "Head Teacher—Mistress Baker." 'Twas my first day at pirate school and my heart quickened as I swung my sea chest upon my shoulder and pushed open the great wooden gates.

But pride turned to dismay at what I saw before me. There were no planks for walk-the-plank classes, no yard-arms from whence to hang one's foes, only a common playground like any other playground full of small groups of young students

garbed in white shirts, red ties, and gray flannel trousers—and horror upon horrors, some of them were playing with yo-yos.

And then I beheld it, fluttering merrily from some unseen mast behind the crumbling school building: a skull and crossbones—the flag which causes every pirate to swell with pride at his calling. I skirted around the school, 'twixt a motley collection of dustbins and a small hut bearing the words "Drama Studio," and there ahead of me was a small harbor, tied to the quay of which was the sweetest two-hundred-ton schooner I had ever seen.

I raced up the gangplank and opened a hatch . . . below decks stunk of skulduggery. Cautiously, I descended a creaky flight of steps into the darkness below. Smoke-stained beams brushed my head, groaning timbers echoed down the gangways. Then, Dee-dump! Dee-dump! Ahead of me I heard an eerie limping sound. Dee-dump! Dee-dump! My blood froze as it approached me. I flattened myself against the greasy oak wall and started as I felt a lump in the small of my back. When my initial terror subsided I discovered it was a door handle. On turning it, a door swung silently open. I stepped into a pitch black cabin and waited. The halting step approached my hiding-place, paused, then moved off again. I was safe.

"Gotcha!" A hand clawed at my face.

"Snoopin' were ye?" Two more hands grabbed my arms and wrenched them tight behind my back, sending my chest crashing to the ground. I was being inspected by two of the foulest young schoolboys I had ever seen. One had the face of a skeleton and spectacles with lenses six inches thick; the other was a pale tallowy creature with a bandage around two fingers of his left hand. I watched in horror as he began to poke my chest.

"Full of bits and baubles, I'll be bound," sneered the other.

"Nay, two silver-handled pistols, a tinder from the Indies, and my father's priceless treasure maps," I retorted recklessly and glanced down at the key I kept secreted on a chain around my neck. In a trice, eight broken fingernails and a bandage tore it from me. I cried out in despair. My first day, and my dearest possessions were to be lost.

At that moment the room flooded with light.

"Near-Sighted Pew! Black Dog!" snapped a haughty buxom woman. "How many times do I have to tell ye, this boat is out of bounds! Now, return the chest and key at once!" Sullenly, the rogues obeyed.

"Sorry, mistress," they whined. "We thought 'e were a-trespassing," and they slunk off into the shadows.

"You must be Ben," continued the head-mistress, for indeed it was she. "Take no heed of Pew. He's a kindly boy, really. Indeed, I have arranged for you to share a study. Come, I'll show you the lie of the land."

We left the schooner and proceeded across the harbor.

"You join us at a time of high excitement," she said proudly. "In order to place the school on a sound financial basis, this quay is to be transformed. In three weeks it will no longer be a grubby backwater, 'twill become 'Squire Trelawney's Pirate World.' Folk will come from far and wide to witness how the world once was when pirates sailed the Spanish Main. In exchange for two pieces of silver they will play at pirates for a whole day with free lunch and a trip around the harbor included."

"Play at pirates!" I protested. "But pirating's a serious business."

"Indeed it is," my headmistress affirmed. "But times have changed, schools have no money, and pirates must learn new skills."

As we entered the school, I saw how she was minded. Her young charges neither drank rum nor sang sea shanties. They were engrossed in books on business studies and property markets, while their teachers lectured them on banking and the law of contracts.

"If my school is to succeed it must produce pirates for today's world," she said. "That is the purpose of modern education."

After exchanging my garb for more suitable gray flannels, she left me outside the door of the odious

Pew. I knocked, swallowed hard, and entered. A figure rocked gently back and forth in a hammock. I waited for a renewed attack upon my chest but none came.

"Shiver me timbers!" chuckled a friendly voice. "It's the new sea pup!" The character who had confronted me was about twelve years old with intelligent eyes and a face like a ham. He pulled himself up in his hammock and took my hand in his firm grasp.

"Short John Silver at your service," he said by way of introduction.

"But I'm to share with Near-Sighted Pew," I stuttered.

"Well, Pew's a slippery swab," he retorted, "and I believe the pair of ye have already had a tidy set-to, so I thought to meself, let honest John be young Ben's shipmate."

I was mightily reassured by this invitation and told my new friend how fearful I was of Pew's designs upon my chest. Lazily, Silver leaned over and pressed a panel in the wall. Silently it slid open to reveal a large hidey-hole.

"Stow it here," he said. "It'll be our little secret, eh? As snug as a crab in a cockleshell."

I sat enthralled while he told me tales of his adventures in the workhouse and at reform school, until a bell sounded and I hastened back to the quay where Mistress Baker was to inform me of my duties. I was a mite aggrieved to discover there was to be no fencing practice nor keelhauling. Instead I was obliged to assist in the construction of a box office for Pirate World. Though I would rather have been swinging across a man-o'-war with a dagger between my teeth, the tasks were pleasing enough, particularly the numbering of the tickets, and by evening, tired and satisfied with my labors, I hastened back to my room eager for more of Silver's yarns. But no smiling face welcomed me. I was greeted only by an empty hidey-hole. Short John's assistance had been in vain.

I scoured the school for assistance or a glimpse of the cowardly Pew, until my searchings were

rewarded by the sight of my two foes scuttling towards the schooner. And in their hands were a hammer, a chisel, and my late father's sea chest.

Across the quay I crept, and once more boarded the ship. A shaft of light from below deck indicated the direction the odious pair had taken. With a cunning knife I had purchased from a captain in the Swiss Army, I prised two planks minutely apart and applied my eye to the hole. Below me was an unforgettable sight: a secret room brimful of pirates' apparel—hats, boots, hooks, and eye patches—and piles of vicious weaponry—cutlasses, scimitars, double-headed boarding axes. And in the midst of this buccaneers' bounty stood Pew and Black Dog hacking at my chest. Then a dreadful familiar sound caused them to arrest their activities. Dee-dump! Dee-dump! The limping figure approached them, obscured by shadows.

"We've a-lifted 'is box, Cap'n," whispered Black Dog.

"That snivelin' sea slug'll be crying 'is-self to sleep for loss of it," added Pew, who was clearly no judge of character. "Our little plan's a-comin' on a treat."

The third figure spoke no words but softly whistled "Fifteen Men on a Dead Man's Chest." My curiosity knew no bounds. Who was this mysterious captain to whom even the most obnoxious schoolboys owed allegiance? I prised my hole wide open to catch a sight of his face, but unluckily at that moment Black Dog, who had resumed chiseling, took a severe blow on the thumb with his hammer. He threw his head back in pain, swearing mightily, and on seeing my face above him redoubled his curses and hurled the hammer in my direction. To my relief its force was broken by an overhanging stuffed parrot and I ran for dear life across the boat. I must find Mistress Baker and warn her that a dastardly plan was being hatched right under her poop deck.

I was about to knock on her study door when a cry from within caused me to pause.

"Spare me, Squire!" The headmistress was weeping uncontrollably.

"'Tis not I, Mistress Baker, 'tis the law," replied a gruff, heartless voice. "If the school cannot make money, it must be closed tomorrow."

"But I'm putting it on a business footing," Mistress Baker cried. "Once Pirate World is opened I will even have the wherewithal to purchase textbooks for the new curriculum."

"Once Pirate World is open," crowed the Squire, "I won't need a school. I'll flatten it and use the site to park the visitors' carriages."

"Wait!" the hapless headmistress pleaded. "I have a new boy, a foolish prig who knows not his head from a packet of lard. He has a sea chest containing a pair of silver pistols. I'll confiscate them and give them to you if only you'll spare my school. What do you say?"

I did not wait to hear the Squire's answer. I was surrounded by villains; even Mistress Baker was after the contents of my chest. I must seek out my one friend in the world—Short John Silver.

I sped to our study and slammed the door behind me.

"Gotcha again!" It was the loathsome voice of Black Dog. I cursed myself for the ass I had been. In my haste I had failed to observe my two

enemies secreted on either side of the entrance.

"The treasure maps—where are they? You took 'em out the box, didn't ye?" hissed Near-Sighted Pew, twisting my arm and causing my eyes to water.

"Aye, that I did. And stored them cunningly where you will never find them," I retorted with all the bravery I could muster.

And then, Dee-dump! Dee-dump! I heard the dread sound approaching like the last judgement.

"'Tis the cap'n," grinned Black Dog wolfishly. "He'll winkle out their whereabouts, by thunder!"

The door opened and, to my amazement, all was revealed. I had never seen Short John Silver standing up before, and there he was, one leg of human flesh, the other completely absent, causing him to walk with the aid of an enormous crutch. And, wonder of wonders, he was carrying my treasure maps.

"How in the name of Lucifer did you find them?" I gasped.

"They were under your pillow, dolt," replied my erstwhile friend. "A drunken cuttlefish could have devised a better hiding place. Take 'em, boys, and if you blab to Mistress Baker, Ben, 'tis Davy Jones' Locker for you."

Fear gripped my heart. I wanted my own locker, not someone else's.

"Mistress Baker would prove no assistance," I retorted. "She too desires my chest. For the Squire will close the school tomorrow unless she finds some means of providing him with money."

"Tomorrow!" exploded my assailants in horror. Then Silver propelled himself out of the room and down the corridor bawling, "Israel Hands, Billy Bones, Job Anderson, stir yourselves from your slumbers! New orders, we sail tonight!"

Even as he spoke, boys burst from their rooms and followed him hotfoot to the ship, discarding their ties, shirts, and flannel trousers as they ran. Soon twenty lads were racing up the gangplank dressed only in their undergarments. Hotfoot I pursued them, desperate for my chest. They dived below deck and in a trice had garbed themselves in their pirate's wear. No longer was I surrounded by school children. Nay, twenty fearsome buccaneers were now swarming up the rigging.

"We had planned this little jaunt for three weeks hence," yelled Short John, who was now miraculously transformed into a pirate captain. "Let modern schooling go hang; what need we of fancy Pirate Worlds when the high seas beckon. May Baker and her business schemes rot in hell. With your treasure maps to guide us we will sail the

seven seas, and bow and scrape to no man. Are you with us, Ben, or shall we toss you to the sharks?"

Before I could consider my answer, I spied Mistress Baker hastening across the quay calling, "Come back, boys—remember your education!" The ship strained at its mooring rope. I lifted a cutlass to hack it through. "Not you too, Ben Gunn," she bellowed. "I have need of your pistols."

I brought the blade down with a crash. The boat swung seaward, the sails billowed, the crew began to sing a haunting pirate melody. Short John Silver put his arm around my shoulder and once more bestowed a smile upon me.

"Ben Gunn," he said, "we'll be the best of mates forever and ever." And looking into his clear blue eyes I knew that he would never let me down.

And was I correct to trust my friend? Read Treasure Island *by Robert Louis Stevenson and discover the answer.*

THE BATTLE IN HOUSEBOAT BAY

Arthur Ransome

This is an extract from Swallows and Amazons, *the first book in the popular series of twelve featuring the adventurous Walker and Blackett children. The Walkers John, Susan, Titty, and Roger, have taken the name Swallows from the small sailboat they are allowed to use while on vacation by a lake. The Amazons are Nancy Blackett and her younger sister Peggy, who have a boat called . . . Amazon, of course! The Swallows and Amazons enjoy a summer of exploration, battles, and alliances, and finally join forces to defeat the greatest enemy of all. To the Swallows and Amazons, a favorite uncle has become none other than Captain Flint, the fiercest buccaneer to sail the seven seas . . . .*

"Let go halyards," John and Nancy shouted almost at the same moment, as *Swallow* and *Amazon* shot up on opposite sides of the houseboat.

"Grab the yard, Susan," shouted John. "Down with it. Hang on to anything you can, Roger, and make the painter fast. Board!"

There was a railing around the houseboat's afterdeck. Captain John swung himself up to the deck by it, climbed over it, and gave a hand to Susan. At that moment Captain Flint, roaring, "Death or Glory!" charged up the companion-way. He had gone down again through the forehatch and run through the cabin. He came up whirling two scarlet cushions around his head. But in hand-to-hand fighting like this it is not weapons that count, but hands. Captain Flint's were large, but he had only two of them. The Swallows' were small, but they had eight.

One tremendous blow of a scarlet cushion caught Captain John on the side of the head, and sent him to the deck. But he was up again in a moment, and charged head down into Captain Flint. Mate Susan had gotten a good hold of one of the cushions. Titty and Roger, who had clambered aboard, took Captain Flint firmly around each leg and clung on like terriers, so that as he moved they dragged with him. Even so, the battle might have ended with the complete defeat of the Swallows if Captain Nancy and her mate, Peggy, who had come aboard by the foredeck, had not rushed along the roof of the cabin and, with a wild yell flung themselves into the struggle. Captain Nancy leaped from the roof of the cabin onto Captain Flint's back, and clasped him around the neck. Peggy joined John and Susan in pulling at him from in front, and, overwhelmed by numbers, Captain Flint came heavily down on the deck.

"Yield," shouted Nancy.

"Not while my flag flies," panted Captain Flint. "Elephants, Elephants, Elephants for ever!"

But Able Seaman Titty was already running forward along the narrow gangway outside the cabin. In another moment, the huge elephant flag came fluttering down to the foredeck.

"We've won," shouted John. "Your flag is struck."

"Why, so it is," said Captain Flint, struggling to a sitting position, and looking at the bare flagstaff. "Quick work. But very hot. I surrender." He lay down flat, puffing heavily.

"Bind him," said Captain Nancy.

Peggy picked up a coil of rope lying handy, and John and Peggy between them bound the prisoner's legs together. Then, with the help of the others, they rolled him over and bound his arms. Then, they tugged him along the deck, and lifted up the top part of him, so that he was sitting on the deck with his back leaning against the cabin. He fell over sideways. John pulled him up again, and he fell over on the other side. "I'll put you up once more," said Peggy, "but, if you roll over again, you shall lie there."

At that moment Titty came back.

"If we're going to make him walk the plank," she said, "there's one all ready on the foredeck."

"So there is," cried Nancy. "I'd forgotten about it. But how are we going to get him there?"

Captain Flint wriggled his feet, and wagged his head from side to side.

"I'm not a snake," he said, "I can't get along without feet."

"We must get him to the foredeck somehow," said Captain Nancy.

"Undo his legs and make him walk over the cabin," said Peggy.

"Cabin roof won't bear me," said the prisoner.

"It's not safe to let prisoners go below," said Titty. "They might set fire to the magazine and blow up the ship."

"We'll take him around by the gangway," said Captain Nancy. "He won't dare to struggle there while his arms are tied."

So they undid the rope from around his legs. With a good deal of difficulty they got him on his feet. He showed signs of sitting down again at once.

"None of that," said Captain Nancy, "or it'll be worse for you. Far worse."

One end of the rope was still wound around and around his arms and body. They made it fast, so that the other end served as a sort of painter or leading string. Nancy and Peggy took hold of the rope, and went first along the narrow gangway. The prisoner, balancing himself as well as he could, walked next. John and Susan followed close behind him. Roger and Titty ran forward over the cabin roof.

On the foredeck there was a capstan, from which the chain went to the big barrel buoy to which the houseboat was moored. There was the little brass cannon. There was the white sun helmet lying by the forehatch. There was a locker close to the little mast at the foot of which on the deck lay the green and white elephant flag. On the starboard side of the deck there was a springboard, from which, on happier days, the owner of the houseboat was accustomed to take his morning dive. It might have been designed for the use of prisoners on their way to feed the sharks. At the sight of it Captain Flint shuddered so violently that he nearly upset the determined buccaneers who had captured him and his ship and were now holding him to prevent any attempt at escape.

"Belay that," growled Captain Nancy. Captain John was really commodore, but in some things Captain Nancy could not help taking the lead.

"Tie the prisoner to the mast," she said, and it was done.

"Don't laugh," she roared at the prisoner.

"Then help that pirate out of my sun helmet," said Captain Flint.

Roger, the boy, had picked up the big sun helmet, and put it on, and the whole of his head was inside it. There was a moment's pause while Mate Susan freed him from it.

"Would you mind putting it on my head," said the prisoner. "A last wish, you know. My bald head can't stand the sun."

Mate Susan put it on for him, and the prisoner, wagging his head, shook it into place.

"Now, Captain John," said Nancy. "We must consider his crimes. The worst is treachery. All this summer he has been in league with the natives."

"Desertion," said Peggy. "He deserted us."

"He came to Wild Cat Island, and went into our camp when we were not there," said Titty.

"He called Captain John a liar," said Nancy.

"That was a mistake," said Captain John hurriedly. "We've made peace over that."

"We can let him off that, then," said Captain Nancy. "But it doesn't matter. His other crimes are quite enough. Hands up for making him walk the plank!"

Her hand and Peggy's went up at once. So did Titty's. So did Roger's. John and Susan hesitated.

"Oh, look here," said Nancy, "no weakening. It's far too good a plank to waste."

"I think we ought to give him a chance," said John. "Untie his arms, and let him swim for it."

"Right," said Nancy. "We'll agree to that. All hands up?"

All hands went up.

Roger was looking over the side.

"Are there plenty of sharks?" he said.

"Millions," groaned the prisoner.

"Bandage his eyes," said Captain Nancy. "Here's a handkerchief."

"A clean one?" asked the prisoner.

"Well, let him have Peggy's. Hers was clean yesterday," said Nancy.

Peggy's handkerchief had not even been unfolded. It was quickly made into a bandage, and tied over Captain Flint's eyes.

"Untie him from the mast, and get him on the plank," said Nancy.

Mate Susan and John loosed him from the mast. Then they unbound his arms. The prisoner swayed heavily this way and that. At last, with Titty and Roger pushing behind, Peggy, John, and Susan between them guided him to the plank. Captain Nancy watched with folded arms.

"Now walk!" she cried.

Captain Flint, blindfolded, moved his feet little by little along the springboard. He stopped, shaking all over, while the springboard bent and quivered under his weight.

Captain Nancy stamped her foot. "Walk, you son of a sea cook," she cried.

Captain Flint took another step or two, until he was at the very end of the plank, high over the water.

"Mercy," he begged. "Mercy!"

"Walk," shouted Nancy, "or . . . !"

Captain Flint stepped desperately forward, taking a long stride into thin air. Head over heels he fell. There was a colossal splash that even wetted the Swallows and Amazons on the deck of the houseboat. Captain Flint had disappeared, and the white sun helmet floated alone, tossing lightly in the ripples.

"Perhaps he can't swim," said Titty. "I never thought of it."

But just then the big bald head of Captain Flint rose out of the water. He blew and spluttered mightily, tore the handkerchief from around his eyes, and sank again.

He came up once more, this time close to the sun helmet. He grabbed it and threw it, spinning, up on the deck of his ship.

"He can swim all right," said Titty.

Suddenly he let loose a yell. "Sharks, sharks!" he shrieked, and, splashing as hard as he could, swam to the houseboat's big mooring buoy. He climbed on to it, though it upset him once or twice. At last he was sitting astride on the top of it.

"This place is stiff with sharks," he called. "One of them's nibbling at my foot."

He slipped sideways off the buoy, and swam to the side of the houseboat, splashing tremendously.

"A rope, a rope!" he shouted, bobbing in the water and splashing with his arms, while the Swallows and Amazons looked down at his struggles.

"Shall we let him have one?" said Susan. "He's been a good long time in the water."

"You'll never be in league with natives again?" said Nancy.

"Hard-hearted pirate, never," said Captain Flint, blowing like a walrus that has come up to breathe.

"We'll give you a rope," said Nancy.

"I'd much rather have a rope ladder," said Captain Flint. "At my age I'm getting too fat for ropes. There's a rope ladder just by the springboard, the plank, I mean. It's made fast. You've only got to throw the loose end overboard."

John threw over the rope ladder, and a moment later Captain Flint stood once more on the deck of his ship with the water pouring from him, and running away into the scuppers. He sat down on the capstan and swung his arms about his chest. "Well, that's that," he said. "Not even the Amazon pirates are ruthless enough to make a man walk the plank twice on one day. Hello, Roger, looking for the sharks?"

Roger had been looking down into the water from the houseboat's deck.

"I don't believe there are any," he said. "None big enough, anyway."

"The young ruffian's sorry I haven't left a leg or an arm behind with them," said Captain Flint. "What are you going to do with me now?" he added. "You've captured my ship, you've hauled down my noble elephant, you've trussed me like a chicken, you've made me walk the plank. I've walked it, dodged the sharks, and come aboard to report for duty. Do you think my crimes are wiped out? Because if they are . . . ." He paused.

"What?" said Captain Nancy.

"All the best sea fights end with a banquet," said

Captain Flint. "And there's one waiting in the cabin and nobody but the parrot on guard there. Just let me go below and start the Primus while I get into some dry things, and then there's nothing to keep us from it."

Nobody had anything to say against that.

Captain Flint lowered himself through the forehatch. A moment later he put his head out.

"By the way," he said. "I suppose you'll want to hoist the Jolly Roger on your prize. You'll find one in the locker." He bobbed down again, and they heard him bumping about below deck. Peggy opened the locker by the mast, and there, on the top, lay a black flag with a skull and crossbones on it as big as the elephant. She and Titty took the elephant flag off the halyards and fastened on the Black Jack. Then, with a cheer from both ships' companies, Peggy ran it to the masthead.

THE MYSTERY
OF THE
PIRATE GHOST

Geoffrey Hayes

One morning in Boogle Bay, Otto and his Uncle Tooth were cleaning their attic.

"What's in that old trunk?" Otto asked.

"Things I brought back from my travels at sea many years ago," Uncle Tooth said.

Uncle Tooth opened the trunk. He took out a shiny silver trumpet. "I found this on Foghorn Island. What an adventure that was!" he said.

"I wish I could have adventures," Otto said. "Nothing ever happens around here."

Uncle Tooth gave Otto the trumpet. "It's yours if you want it," he said.

"Gee, thanks!" said Otto.

Otto blew on the trumpet. Nothing happened. He took a big breath and blew again. This time the trumpet made a little "fwee" sound.

"Keep trying," Uncle Tooth said, "and you will get it right."

Otto ran outside with his trumpet.

Uncle Tooth's sister, Auntie Hick, was hurrying down the path. She did not see Otto.

"Fwee!" went the trumpet.

Auntie Hick screamed. Uncle Tooth came running.

"I'm sorry, Auntie Hick," said Otto. "I was just playing."

"Playing, my foot!" said Auntie Hick. "I thought you were the ghost!"

"What ghost?" cried Otto.

"The ghost in my shop," she said. "This morning I heard noises inside my shop. I opened the door and saw—a ghost! It stared at me with big red eyes! I ran here as fast as I could."

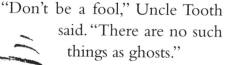

"Don't be a fool," Uncle Tooth said. "There are no such things as ghosts."

Auntie Hick stamped her foot. "I say there are, because I've just seen one."

Otto jumped up and down. "Let's go find the ghost," he said. "This might be the start of an adventure."

The three of them hurried up the path toward Auntie Hick's shop.

They passed Captain Poopdeck's houseboat. The captain was on deck. He was picking up wet laundry.

"Of all the rotten things," he muttered.

"What's wrong?" asked Uncle Tooth.

"Someone stole my clothesline," said the captain.

"I'll bet anything it was the ghost!" said Auntie Hick.

"What ghost?" cried the captain.

"There's a ghost on the loose in Boogle Bay," said Otto. "And we're going to catch it!"

"Wait for me," said the captain. "I'll join you."

Soon they came to the inn.

Joe Puffin was standing on a stool in front of the door. He had a cigar in one hand and a scrub brush in the other. He was screeching loudly.

"What's the matter, Joe?" asked Uncle Tooth.

"Someone broke in here last night," said the puffin. "They turned everything upside down. Then they did this."

He pointed to the door. On it was a big red skull and crossbones.

"I'm sure it was the ghost," said Auntie Hick.

Otto told the puffin about the ghost. "We're gong to catch it. Want to help?"

"Count me in," said Joe Puffin.

They tiptoed to Auntie Hick's shop. Uncle Tooth opened the door. They peeked in.

Auntie Hick screamed.

There were boxes and jars, gumdrops and jelly beans, all over the floor. But there was no ghost.

"This ghost loves to make messes," said Uncle Tooth.

"Some detective you are!" said Auntie Hick. "Any fool can see that!"

Then she began counting boxes. "The ghost is a thief," she said. "It took five boxes of saltwater taffy and a deck of cards. This is serious. What are you going to do about it, Tooth?"

"I am going to the inn," he said. "Food always helps me think."

Back at the inn, Joe Puffin served up bowls of his special carrot soup.

"Delicious!" said Uncle Tooth. "Now, how will we catch this ghost? A thief returns to the scene of the crime."

"Do ghosts return, too?" asked Otto.

"We will see," said Uncle Tooth. "We need something to lure it into our trap."

"I know," Otto said. "My trumpet!"

"Good thinking, Otto," said his uncle. "Now, here is what we will do . . . ."

That night Otto put his trumpet on the street outside the inn. The trumpet shone in the moonlight. Then Otto crawled inside a barrel. Uncle Tooth hid in a doorway. Captain Poopdeck crouched behind the bar at the inn. And Joe Puffin flew up to the roof with a fish net.

Midnight came and went.

Otto crept out of the barrel and peeked around the corner. He saw a giant shadow. Was it the ghost?

No! It was Uncle Tooth.

"Shush!" Uncle Tooth whispered. "The ghost is coming."

Otto held his breath.

The ghost bent down and picked up the shiny silver trumpet.

"Now!" yelled Uncle Tooth. Then he and Otto raced around the corner.

Captain Poopdeck turned on the lights in the inn. The puffin flew from the roof and dropped the fishnet over the ghost. The ghost slipped free of the net. It ran down a dark alley. Everyone chased it.

Then it disappeared!

Uncle Tooth scratched his head. "Well, if that doesn't beat all!" he said. "Maybe the thief really is a ghost."

"Look!" cried Otto. He pointed to an open manhole in the street.

Otto stuck his lantern down the manhole. He saw something! It was bobbing up and down in the water. Otto climbed down a ladder and fished it out with his sword.

"A pirate's hat!" cried Uncle Tooth. "This looks like old Blackeye Doodle's hat to me."

"Didn't Blackeye drown at sea?" asked Joe Puffin.

"That he did," said Uncle Tooth. "But it would be just like him to come back from the dead to haunt us."

"And now he has my trumpet," said Otto sadly.

"We'll get it back," said Uncle Tooth. "Tomorrow we will visit Widow Mole at Deadman's Landing. She used to work for Blackeye. Maybe she can give us some clues. But now let's get some sleep. I am as tired as an old boot."

The next morning Otto was up early. He came downstairs with his sword, a map, a lantern, and a spyglass.

"You look all set for ghost hunting," said Uncle Tooth.

He opened the door.

"Look!" cried Otto.

There was a note pinned to the door with a knife! Otto read it:

GIVE ME BACK MY HAT
OR YOU WILL BE SORRY!

It was signed "Blackeye Doodle."

Uncle Tooth snorted. "I have seen many strange things in my day," he said. "But I never saw a note from a ghost before."

Uncle Tooth rowed his boat down the coast.

Otto looked through his spyglass. But the fog was so thick he could not see anything. "This is spooky," he said.

"You are not scared, are you?" asked Uncle Tooth.

"Of course not," said Otto.

Soon they heard the tinkling sound of a piano through the fog. They rounded a bend and docked at Widow Mole's Pool Hall.

Uncle Tooth and Otto swung the door open and marched in. The pool hall was filled with mean-looking sailors. Some were playing pool. Some were drinking beer. Widow Mole was at the piano.

"Tooth! As I live and breathe!" she cried. "What brings you here?"

"A ghost," said Uncle Tooth.

Widow Mole stopped playing the piano. The pool hall got very quiet. Uncle Tooth showed Widow Mole the pirate's hat.

"It's Blackeye's hat, all right," she said. "He was a

mean pirate, but a good friend. I'm sorry he is gone."

"We are not so sure he is gone," said Uncle Tooth. "He might even be here—on Deadman's Landing. He used to hide out here, didn't he?"

"Yes," said Widow Mole. "In a cave. But I don't know where. It was his secret."

"Thanks," said Uncle Tooth. "We will have a look around."

Otto and Uncle Tooth walked outside—and fell onto the dock! Blackeye's hat flew out of Otto's hands.

The ghost grabbed the hat, put it on, and faded into the fog.

"What happened?" asked Otto.

Uncle Tooth pointed to the door.

"See that rope across the doorway?" he said. "It is Captain Poopdeck's clothesline. We were tripped up by a ghost! You wait here for me, Otto. I am going to catch that ghost once and for all!"

He took the clothesline and headed for the beach.

Otto sat on the dock, but he soon got tired of waiting. "I will walk down the beach just a little way," he thought.

After a while Otto found a playing card stuck to a bush. He moved the bush aside and saw a little cave! A bat flew out.

"Having an adventure is scarier than I thought," he said. Otto held out his sword, turned on his lantern, and slowly walked into the cave.

What a surprise!

In a corner of the cave were a bed and a trunk. On the bed were playing cards and candy wrappers. On the trunk was Otto's trumpet.

Suddenly Otto heard a bloodcurdling laugh. He turned around. The ghost was watching him with its big red eyes! Otto was trapped.

The eyes came nearer and nearer. Otto grabbed the trumpet and blew on it as hard as he could.

"BLAAT!" went the trumpet.

The trumpet was so loud and so surprising that the ghost jumped and ran out of the cave. It was so loud that Uncle Tooth heard it.

He came running down the beach. "Otto! Are you all right?" he shouted.

"Y-y-yes," Otto said. "But the ghost got away."

"There it is!" cried Uncle Tooth. He pointed to the rocks above. Otto looked up. Something black peeked over the top of the rocks.

"It's Blackeye's hat! After it!" cried Uncle Tooth.

They climbed up the rocks. But just as they got near the top, the ghost stood up and jumped off the cliff!

Uncle Tooth and Otto raced to the edge and looked over. In a cove below was a half-sunken old ship. The ghost was running across the deck.

Suddenly there was a loud CRACK! The rotten wood broke apart. The ghost fell through the deck and—SPLASH!—right into the water.

Something else was splashing in the water nearby.

"An octopus!" cried Otto.

"Help!" screamed the ghost. "Don't let it get me!"

Uncle Tooth threw the clothesline down. The ghost grabbed it. Otto and Uncle Tooth began to pull him up. The pirate's hat fell off and landed on the octopus.

"Looks like Blackeye's hat has found a new owner," said Uncle Tooth.

A very wet ghost stood before them.

"Now, take off that silly costume. We know you are Blackeye Doodle," Uncle Tooth said.

"No, I'm not," said the ghost. He took off his ghost costume. "I'm his son, Ducky Doodle. And I'm twice as tough as my pa."

"We'll see how tough you are in jail," Uncle Tooth said.

Ducky Doodle's face fell.

"Don't send me to jail," he begged. "Life in the orphanage was bad enough. I ran away to be a pirate like my pa."

Uncle Tooth shook his head. "Listen, Doodle, a pirate's life is nothing but trouble. So far, you have upset people. You have stolen things. And you even lost your father's hat."

"I'm sorry," said Ducky Doodle. "But I don't know what else to do."

"Otto and I will show you how to earn an honest living," said Uncle Tooth.

"Okay," said Ducky Doodle. "I will give it a try."

Ducky Doodle did not go to jail. But he did pay for his crimes. First he returned the clothesline to Captain Poopdeck—and washed a tub of dirty laundry.

Next he told Joe Puffin that he was sorry. Joe Puffin forgave Doodle, but only after Doodle washed the dishes and scrubbed the floor.

Then Otto, Uncle Tooth, and Ducky Doodle went to Auntie Hick's shop.

"This is the ghost," Uncle Tooth said. He told Auntie Hick the whole story.

"Well, I never!" Auntie Hick said.

"I will pay you back by working in your shop," said Ducky Doodle.

Auntie Hick thought about that. "Well, I sure could use some help," she told Otto and Uncle Tooth. "I'll see that he behaves himself, and I'll teach him to read and write. I'm sure he didn't learn much in the orphanage."

Ducky Doodle groaned.

Auntie Hick let Otto and Uncle Tooth keep the rest of the stolen candy.

"It's not much of a reward," Otto said. "But we had fun."

"More fun than mending fishnets," said Uncle Tooth. "Maybe we could solve more mysteries."

"And have more adventures!" cried Otto.

So they did!

TREASURE ISLAND

Robert Louis Stevenson
An extract retold by Joyce Faraday

The most famous pirate story of all, Treasure Island *begins when young Jim Hawkins comes into possession of a map showing where a certain wicked pirate, Captain Flint, buried his treasure. Jim shows it to Dr. Livesey and Squire Trelawney, and together they set out by ship to find the treasure. But their crew includes several ex-members of Flint's pirate crew, among them Long John Silver who leads a mutiny. Jim has many adventures, including an encounter with Ben Gunn, a wild man who was marooned on the island by Flint. In this extract, Jim finds himself with Silver and the surviving pirates searching for the treasure. But a surprise is in store for them all . . . .*

With picks and shovels, we set out to find Captain Flint's treasure. The men were armed to the teeth. Silver had two guns and a cutlass. As I was a prisoner, I had a rope tied around my waist. Silver held the other end. In spite of his promise to keep me safe, I did not trust him.

As we went, the men talked about the chart.

On the back of it was written:

*"Tall tree, Spyglass Shoulder, bearing a point
to the N. of N.N.E.
Skeleton Island E.S.E. and by E.
Ten feet."*

So we were looking for a tall tree on a hill. The men were in high spirits, and Silver and I could not keep up with them.

Suddenly there was a shout from one of the men in front. The others ran toward him, full of hope. But it was not treasure he had found. At the foot of the tree lay a human skeleton.

The men looked down in horror. The few rags of clothing that hung on the bones showed that the man had been a sailor. The skeleton was stretched out straight, the feet pointing one way and the arms, raised above the head, pointing in the opposite direction.

"This here's one of Flint's little jokes!" cried Silver. "These bones point E.S.E. and by E. This is one of the men he killed, and he's laid him here to point the way!"

The men felt a chill in their hearts, for they had all lived in fear of Flint. "But he's dead," said one of them.

"Aye, sure enough, he's dead and gone below," said another pirate. "But if ever a ghost walked, it would be Flint's."

"Aye," said a third man. "I tell you, I don't like to hear 'Fifteen Men' sung now, for it was the only song he ever sang."

Silver put an end to their talk and we moved on, but I noticed that now the men spoke softly and kept together. Just the thought of Flint was enough to fill them with terror.

At the top of the hill we rested. In whispers, the men still talked of Flint.

"Ah, well," said Silver, "you praise your stars he's dead."

Suddenly, from the trees ahead, a thin, trembling

voice struck up the well-known song:

"Fifteen men on the Dead Man's Chest—
Yo-ho-ho, and a bottle of rum!"

I have never seen men so dreadfully affected as
these pirates. The men were rooted to the spot.
The color drained from their faces as they stared
ahead in terror. Even Silver was shaking, but he was
the first to pull himself together.

"I'm here to get that treasure!" he roared. "I was
never feared of Flint in his life, and by the Powers,
I'll face him dead!"

Long John Silver gave
them all fresh heart, and
they picked up their tools
and set off again.

We soon saw ahead a
huge tree that stood high
above the others. The
thought of what lay near
that tree made the men's
fears fade, and they moved
faster. Silver hobbled on
his crutch. I could tell
from the evil in his eyes
that, if he got his hands on
the gold, he would cut all
our throats and sail away.

The men now broke into a run, but not for long. They had come to the edge of a pit. At the bottom lay bits of wood and the broken handle of a pickax. It was clear for all to see that the treasure had gone!

The pirates jumped down into the hole and began to dig with their hands. Silver knew that they would turn on him at any moment.

"We're in a tight spot, Jim," he whispered. The look of hate in his eyes had gone. With the pirates against him, he needed me again. Once more he had changed sides.

The pirates scrambled out of the pit and stood facing Silver and me. The leader raised his arm to charge, but before a blow was struck, three musket shots rang out and two pirates fell. The three men left ran for their lives. From out of the wood ran the doctor and Ben Gunn, who had saved us in the nick of time.

Silver and I were taken to Ben Gunn's cave, where the rest of our party was waiting. It was a happy moment for me to see all my friends again. And my friends were glad to move out of the log house to the safety of Gunn's cave.

We now learned the answer to the question that had puzzled Silver and me. Dr. Livesey had found out that Ben Gunn, alone on the island for so long, had discovered the treasure and taken it to his cave. The map, then, was useless.

That morning, Ben Gunn had watched from the woods as the pirates set out to seek the treasure. It was *his* voice that had struck terror into their hearts with his ghostly song!

That night the captain, still weak from his wounds, along with Squire Trelawney, Dr. Livesey, and the rest of us, feasted and laughed and rested. Long John Silver, smiling quietly, became the polite and willing seaman I had first known.

The next day we began to pack the treasure into sacks, in preparation for loading it aboard the *Hispaniola*. There was a great mass of gold coins, from every part of the world, and transporting it

all was a difficult task. It took several days to move this great fortune. With the treasure stowed, and plenty of water, we were ready to weigh anchor and set sail for home.

Though we were not certain of their whereabouts, we knew there were three pirates still on the island. After some deliberation, we decided to leave them a good stock of food, along with some medicine, clothing, and tools, so that they could last until some ship found them.

And so we set sail. I cannot express the joy I felt as I watched Treasure Island melt into the distance and disappear over the horizon.

THE PIRATE QUEEN

Emily Arnold McCully

Long ago, when Ireland was all untamed, the greatest captain and pirate of the age sailed forth from Connaught in the west. Grania O'Malley was her name.

For centuries O'Malleys pulled lobster, herring, and salmon from the coiling seas. Their cattle dotted the meadows ashore. Most sailors were pirates if they got the chance, and O'Malleys were no different.

When the clan elected Owen O'Malley their chief, he was a wealthy man. His daughter was born at their Clare Island castle in 1530. Owen lifted the infant in his arms and his wife remarked, "Look, she has the light of the sea in her eye."

The friars taught Grania to read Latin sitting beneath the O'Malley motto, *Terra Mariq Potens*— Invincible on Land and Sea. As soon as she could

tie a knot, Grania begged to sail with the fleet. Her mother said it was no life for a young girl, but Grania wouldn't give up. She ran off and returned with her hair shorn like a boy's. Her parents laughed at her willfulness and nicknamed her Grania the Bald. She had won the right to go to sea.

Owen taught Grania the ways of the lashing tides and the siren winds. Soon every cranny along the coast was familiar, and she was at home on the black deep. When the horizon was empty of ships, Grania could outdance the nimblest sailor and outgamble him, too.

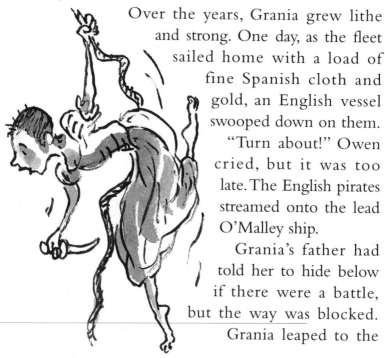

Over the years, Grania grew lithe and strong. One day, as the fleet sailed home with a load of fine Spanish cloth and gold, an English vessel swooped down on them.

"Turn about!" Owen cried, but it was too late. The English pirates streamed onto the lead O'Malley ship.

Grania's father had told her to hide below if there were a battle, but the way was blocked. Grania leaped to the rigging and scrambled up. She saw her father stumble across the deck, wounded. Behind him an English pirate raised his dagger. Shrieking an Irish curse, Grania pounced.

The Englishman went down. "It's a maiden!" the pirates cried in awe.

"Aye, and she's ours!" shouted the O'Malley crew. They fought ferociously until the English were captured and in chains.

By the force of her courage, a sea queen was born.

When she was sixteen, it was time for Grania to marry, as all girls did. She and her parents chose hot-tempered Donal O'Flaherty, of another seafaring clan. Grania was soon in charge of the O'Flaherty fleet. Under her command, ships patrolled the outer islands, extracting a fee for the use of the waters. If a captain refused to pay, she gave the signal and her men removed the cargo. She was as brave as the stoutest of her followers and they loved her for that.

Grania's first son was born on the high seas. She named him Owen, after her father. When Turkish pirates attacked her galley the next day, the mate scurried down to fetch her.

"What?" She laughed. "You can't do without me for a single day!"

She exchanged the babe for a blunderbuss, put it

under her cape, and burst on to the deck. There she danced a wild jig, freezing the Turks in their tracks. Grania whipped out her blunderbuss and fired it off. The Turks dove over the gunwales.

Grania loved this life, hard as it was.

Throughout the marriage, Donal fought brawls until he met his end at the hands of a rival clan. Grania was entitled to a widow's portion of his property, but the O'Flahertys refused to give it to her. So Grania hired a new crew consisting of men who loved cards and dice as much as she did. "Grania of the Gamblers," many called her.

They established a base at Clare Island, her childhood home. There, piece by piece, she built her sea kingdom.

When Grania had five castles, she controlled all

but the northeast side of Clew Bay. There stood stout Rockfleet Castle with its inland harbor. Grania had her eye on it, too. From Rockfleet she would be able to see any ship that entered the bay. To its safety she could scurry from attackers on the open sea. The more she considered Rockfleet, the more she had to have it. She thought of a way.

Rockfleet belonged to Richard Burke, known as Richard-in-Iron. One day Grania strode up to his door and said, "Let us marry. We two can withstand any invasion the English may send." Richard-in-Iron was delighted to accept Grania's proposal. The sixth and finest castle was now hers.

But Richard, like Donal before him, proved more hotheaded than shrewd. He mounted a rebellion against the Duke of Desmond. Grania had no quarrel with the duke, but she went along for Richard's sake. Everyone who saw her in action was awestruck. She flew into the thick of battle, knocking knights off their steeds. But in the end she was outnumbered and the duke captured her.

Never before confined by anyone, Grania was thrown into prison in Limerick. The dungeon was miserable and she longed to be free, but her spirit never faltered. After a year and a half, the Lord Justice in Dublin unexpectedly sent for her.

"I will release you, Grania O'Malley," he said, but you must promise to end your career of pirating and marauding."

What could she say? Grania said she would. Her heart knew otherwise.

She returned to Connaught, determined to be a pirate again. Richard-in-Iron had died a natural death while Grania was in prison. Now she would reside alone at Rockfleet.

But in London, Queen Elizabeth I dispatched a ruthless new governor, Sir Richard Bingham, to subdue the Irish. He hanged or massacred all who resisted the new English laws. Bingham had heard of the famous woman pirate and was determined to destroy her. He began by sending his forces to find her son, Owen.

Owen innocently offered the soldiers hospitality, but they accused him of hiding rebels, tied him up, and murdered him. Then they made off with his herd of cattle.

Grania wept bitterly, but before she could plot her revenge, a strange letter arrived from Sir Richard Bingham himself. Given the unrest, he wrote, she must come and live under his protection.

She hadn't the power to make war on the English governor. It seemed there was no choice but to go as Sir Richard ordered. Grania set forth with her men and herds. Before two days were out, they were ambushed by none other than Sir Richard's soldiers. His safe passage was a lie! Her cattle and mares were stolen, her followers

scattered. The pirate queen was tied up like an animal.

When she was brought to Sir Richard, he pointed to a gallows. "I've had this made just for you, Grania O'Malley," he said. "You'll die tomorrow."

But that evening a powerful Irish lord rode up and asked that Grania be spared. "I give my word," he said. "She will never be pirate nor rebel again."

Sir Richard gave her a sneering glance. "Why not spare you?" he mused. "There's nothing left of you, Grania O'Malley. Your men, your herds, your castles are gone. From what I hear, your ships are all broken as well. Go back to Clew Bay."

Grania hastened to see if Bingham had uttered the truth this time. She found a sorry scene. Her fleet had been broken in a storm, Clew Bay and Galway were controlled by English ships. Her sea kingdom was no more. Only the Clare Island castle was hers.

On the great cliffs that had been the seat of her power, the old sea queen pondered. After decades of fighting, her enemy Bingham now was the most powerful man in Ireland. What's more, his tactics were vicious and cruel. But who sat above Bingham, with greater might even than his? Another woman warrior—the Queen of England!

Grania would demand justice of Elizabeth I.

So Grania O'Malley decided to go to London and see the queen in person. Her loyal followers begged her not to go. No Irish chieftain had dared set foot on English soil. Nothing in Elizabeth's reign vexed her more than the Irish. And when vexed, she had been known to scold people, slap them, and cut off their heads.

When Grania was brought before the Queen, she stated her case in Latin, the only language they shared.

Elizabeth asked how the troubles in Ireland might be ended. "Sir Richard Bingham's brutality makes the people rebel all the more," Grania replied. Elizabeth frowned, and whispered to one of her advisors.

Grania offered to "harry the Queen's enemies with fire and sword on land and sea." If Elizabeth accepted her offer, Grania would be back in business —and Sir Richard could do nothing about it.

Then Grania sneezed.

A lady-in-waiting handed her a handkerchief of embroidered cambric lace. Grania blew noisily.

"Oh!" the courtiers gasped as she tossed it into the fireplace.

The Queen's hard eyes flashed. "Is this what you think of our fine English cloth?" she said. "It was meant for your pocket."

"What?" said Grania, astonished. "In Ireland we value cleanliness more than to put a soiled thing in

our pocket." A terrible silence followed. The Queen frowned darkly. Everyone waited to hear her pronounce the death sentence on the rude Irish pirate. Elizabeth's mouth twitched. She laughed. After a startled moment, the courtiers laughed. Grania laughed. The great chamber rocked with mirth.

"Your customs may be strange," the Queen declared, "but you have led your people bravely. I accept your offer to defend the Crown with fire and sword. Also I grant you maintenance from your husbands' lands."

She had won! Grania made a bow of thanks and the court applauded. The meeting of queens was over.

Grania returned to Ireland, fitted up a fleet, and was soon a pirate again. Bingham did his best to ruin her, but she was more than his match. Grania O'Malley died, for all we know, at the helm of a galley, in the thick of a fight.

THE TALE OF THE BAD SHIP *TORMENT*

Sara Conkey

It was dawn on board the bad ship *Torment*. Captain Razelbreath raised a telescope to his one good eye. The sea was blue and empty: the *Torment* was alone on the wicked high seas. Captain Razelbreath lowered the telescope and laughed his especially terrible laugh. It was a cross between a vulture's cry and a creaky wardrobe door, and if you have never heard that, it is pretty terrible. For Captain Razelbreath had made a huge fortune by terrorizing his way around the oceans of the world. If other ships spied the bad ship *Torment* in the distance, they quickly scooted off in the opposite direction. Razelbreath ruled supreme and that was the way he liked it.

Quickly, Razelbreath made his creaky way into the bowels of the ship. Down and down he went, past the snores of the still sleeping sailors.

135

Finally, he stopped at the deepest, darkest door. He looked to the right and to the left, then pulled out a long thin key on a chain from underneath his long thin cloak.

In a flash he was inside.

The room was dim for it was lit only by a tiny porthole and a candle. It was in this room that the captain kept his one and only love: the Princess Marie-Rose. He had stolen her on a stormy night from the ship of a duke, and of all his treasures, it was she whom he prized the most. But despite all his best attempts, the princess had ignored him from the day she had been captured. She had eaten nothing, although Razelbreath arranged for the most tempting food to be brought to her. She had only said, "I cannot eat and I cannot love."

Marie-Rose was sitting, as she always sat, in a chair of cream, dressed in a dress of dark green silk. Her dark eyes were fixed on the one patch of blue glowing in the only porthole.

It infuriated Razelbreath beyond belief that she could ignore him so completely. For if there's one thing a cruel and heartless sea captain cannot stand, it's to be ignored. Razelbreath liked a lot of attention. He threw a chair at the wall, he threw a cushion at the ceiling and stamped his foot very, very hard. But Marie-Rose sat perfectly still in her green silk dress and simply said, "I cannot eat and I cannot love."

Razelbreath growled, "Have it your way!" And in a flash he had locked the door again.

Razelbreath always kept the key to the princess's room on a chain around his neck, for the captain had a secret and deadly fear.

When he was seven and practicing his wickedness by tormenting toads, he met an old woman whose pet toad he had just mangled in a rather disgusting way. The old woman was so furious she put a curse on Razelbreath: "Wicked you want to be and wicked you shall be, Morton Razelbreath, but if the one you love loves another, before you persuade her to marry you, the spell of your fear will be broken and you will become as small and unimportant as that toad you so cruelly tormented."

Razelbreath shuddered when he remembered the witch's words—as he did every morning—and he was clutched by the iron hand of fear.

"If she loves another . . . ," he whispered. But no, that was impossible, for she saw no one and the only key was around his own scrawny neck.

She will stay there until she loves me—or starves! Razelbreath thought, as he reached the top of the stairs and smiled horribly.

"Work harder or you'll be a shark's breakfast!" he bawled and kicked a sailor who was scrubbing the deck.

The crew of the bad ship *Torment* hated and feared Captain Razelbreath. Quite often he would say, "Work harder or you'll be a shark's breakfast!" and then have a poor sailor thrown overboard just to prove he meant it. The sharks followed the *Torment* all over the wicked high seas, because they knew it was a good meal ticket. And so the crew worked harder and harder, and shivered when Razelbreath passed creakily by.

But there was one crew member who was not afraid of Captain Razelbreath. His name was Simon and he was the assistant cook.

He was the smallest and youngest of the crew members. Simon completely ignored Razelbreath's rages: he merely sighed and carried on cooking. For Simon was secretly a master chef: he was forced to cook the stews and soups of sailors' fare, but he dreamed of one day making cherry flans and strawberry fools and scrumptious salads.

At that moment, the captain burst into the kitchen. Simon had just made a plateful of steaming ginger and cinnamon biscuits and proceeded to get them out of the oven. Razelbreath watched the boy with his one good eye.

"Stand still boy, or you'll be a shark's breakfast!"

"Yes, Captain," replied Simon. "I just thought you might like to try a biscuit."

He held one out to the captain.

The captain snatched the biscuit from the boy's hand and gobbled it in one terrible gulp. Then a curious expression spread over the captain's face: somewhere between a grimace and a glare. He grabbed the plateful of biscuits and tipped them into his mouth and down his throat in one go. In two seconds they were all gone, with only a few crumbs left on the plate to show they had ever been.

Razelbreath wiped his mouth with his one good arm and eyed the boy carefully. He had thought of a cunning and terrible plan.

"Boy, make three irresistible meals by sundown or you'll be a shark's supper." And with that he made his creaky way out of the kitchen. Simon could hardly believe his luck! A free hand to cook what he liked! So while Simon weighed and rolled and sieved and chopped, the captain paced and grunted and sniggered and growled, and somewhere far, far below in the bowels of the ship, the Princess Marie-Rose stared at the only porthole and sighed a large sigh.

The sun had set. Razelbreath creaked into the kitchen. He half hoped the boy hadn't succeeded in making the three irresistible meals, for then he could throw him to the sharks. But Simon was standing there with three platters covered in linen cloths.

The captain pulled back the first cloth. A riot of colour invaded his one good eye—it was a ship made of every kind of fruit you could possibly

imagine—golden peaches were the planks, strings of sliced apples were the ropes, half melons were the sails, and a perfect strawberry the anchor. Razelbreath's eyes were as big as plums.

Quickly, he pulled away the next cloth to reveal a small and perfect turkey, bathed in honey, succulent and juicy beyond imagining. Razelbreath sniffed in ecstasy.

The third platter revealed a pie—and what a pie! It looked as if it was made of clouds. It was swirly and curly like a soft white sea. It smelt of lemons and heaven. A silver spoon lay beside it, invitingly. Razelbreath sighed.

But instead of tucking in without further ado, to Simon's surprise the captain re-covered the food, whisked away the platters and disappeared from the kitchen. He returned an hour later with the empty platters, growling the words, "Boy, make three irresistible meals by tomorrow sundown, or you'll be a shark's supper."

And so it went on, day after day: Simon cooked and baked and stirred—Razelbreath entered and swooned with delight, whisked away the food, and returned with the same instructions. But Simon was exceedingly curious. Who was eating his delicious food?

So the next night when Razelbreath had taken away the three platters, Simon followed him. It was dark on the ship, so the captain did not notice Simon's stealthy footsteps and slim shadow. He slipped through the side door just behind the captain. Down and down they went—Simon had never been so deep into the ship before. At last, around the deepest and darkest bend, the captain stopped. He drew out a long silver key which glittered in the early moonlight. Then he was gone. Simon leaned against the wooden wall, his breath coming hard. He knew that if he was caught, he would be fed to the sharks piece by piece for breakfast, dinner, and supper. But still he had to know.

Silently, he crept up to the door and lowered his eye to the keyhole. And there he saw a sight that made his elbows quiver and his knees melt: the most beautiful girl he had ever seen was delicately spooning his turtleshell soup into her delicate pink rosebud mouth.

Her dark eyes were sparkling with happiness as she tasted the hundred subtle flavors. Her dark thick hair seemed to get thicker and darker, and her white cheeks, starved of sunlight for so long, glowed fresh pink.

Razelbreath was watching her, greedily.

But when she had eaten the last morsel of walnut cake, the princess pushed away the platter, turned and stared at the handful of stars she could see through her only porthole, and said, "I cannot love." Razelbreath smiled his most horrible smile. He had succeeded in making the princess eat—it was just a matter of time before he made her love! He fell to his knees and begged her to marry him. But the princess only said, "I cannot love," and ignored him as completely as if he were invisible.

Simon sped back to the kitchens—and not a moment too soon. Razelbreath creaked through the door, flung the platters on the floor, and growled, "Three irresistible meals by sundown, or you'll be a shark's supper."

But Simon was inspired! Now he had seen the princess he pushed himself to greater and greater heights. Everything he made, he made with the image of Marie-Rose before his eyes. Every pot of cream he whipped, he whipped with love. He made swans of icing sugar, gingerbread flowers, houses made of treacle cake, and orange blancmange cats. And whatever he made, the Princess Marie-Rose ate.

He made hearts of strawberries, baskets of apricots, chocolate faces, and apple crumble. And whatever he made, the Princess Marie-Rose tucked into.

He made boats of ice cream, elephants of marzipan, cherry lemonade, and blueberry pie. And everything he made, the Princess Marie-Rose polished off.

Now love is a strange thing. People can say "I love you" until they are blue in the face and sometimes they mean it and sometimes they don't. But when someone cooks with love, you can taste it straight away.

And so it was with Marie-Rose. When she sipped Simon's cherry lemonade, she knew he loved her. When she tasted his orange blancmange, she knew he adored her, and when she tucked into his blueberry pie, she knew he worshiped her. Each main course was a love letter and each pudding a love song. And she began to melt.

The day this happened was at dawn one summer morning. Razelbreath was making his creaky way down to check that his princess was still safely under lock and key when he began to feel a little shaky. He took another step and began to feel a little quaky. He sat down on a step and felt sick.

Razelbreath was no fool. He knew something had happened. The princess's heart was melting.

Razelbreath began to think hard—how could anyone have got to Marie-Rose? He kept her locked in the deepest, darkest part of the ship, and he kept the only key around his own scrawny neck. He took every morsel of delicious food to her with his own hands, and watched her eat it all alone.

Suddenly Razelbreath saw black. He got up, he raged, he ranted.

He cried out, "I have been far too nice for far too long!"

Then he stormed down the stairs to the deepest darkest door and opened it with a cry. He grabbed Marie-Rose roughly and forced her out of the door and up the wooden steps. On the deck in the bright sunshine, Marie-Rose tottered and almost fell. Razelbreath grasped her roughly to his thin side. He called all the crew to him. They stood quaking before him.

"Today," he announced, "the Princess Marie-Rose and I are going to be married."

The crew gasped.

"We will have a huge wedding breakfast and we'll eat and drink all day."

The crew cheered.

"But first," Razelbreath smiled his most vicious smile, "our fishy friends must share our wedding celebrations."

With that he grabbed Simon by the collar with his one good arm and fixed him with his one good eye.

"It is a pity, my boy, that it will not be your apple crumble we shall be scoffing on my wedding day—" then he whispered in the boy's ear, "The princess has grown to love your pies and pastries— soon she will love you. But sadly, before that happens, we will be married and you will be a shark's indigestion." Throwing Simon to the ground, he growled, "Get the plank."

Meanwhile, the Princess Marie-Rose was growing accustomed to the sunlight. She looked around her at the crew of the bad ship *Torment* scurrying this way and that. And she saw Simon, standing brave and alone, with his hands tied, and although she pitied the young man, she hadn't the faintest clue who he was.

Simon was thrust onto the plank. The sharks circled hungrily beneath. The sea was dark and choppy.

"Walk!" growled Razelbreath.

Simon took a step forward. He looked at the sea, he looked at the sky and finally he looked back at the beautiful Princess Marie-Rose.

He cried out, "I have a last request."

148

Razelbreath sighed.

"Okay. But make it snappy."

Simon took a deep breath. "I would like a syrupy treacle and cinnamon pudding."

"Denied," said Razelbreath. "Get on with your stroll."

"Very well," said Simon, taking another step, "I would like a boat made of chocolate chip and coconut ice cream."

"To sail away in, I suppose?" laughed Razelbreath cruelly. "Don't waste my time, I'm getting hungry."

Simon took a final step, and cried, "I would like a cake made of snow white cream, tasting of lemon and heaven."

"Please Captain Razelbreath, save him!" cried the voice of Marie-Rose. "I will marry you gladly, only save his life—for I love him."

But the wicked Captain Razelbreath only replied, "Croak!"

For he had turned that instant into a small and insignificant toad, destined to be ignored forevermore.

There was a wedding feast on the *Torment* that day —it was for Simon and the Princess Marie-Rose. Simon cooked the most amazing feast and the sailors were quite happy to accept him as their new captain—they had never liked the old one.

And the new captain's skill as a chef spread far and wide: ships for miles around came to sample the excellent cuisine on board the good ship *Torment*. The crew made wonderful waiters. Even the sharks still hung around because the scraps were so tasty.

As for Razelbreath the Toad, he lived in a tiny cage on the deck, and was fed tiny, beautiful meals which he would gobble up in one mouthful and then croak for attention, which he never received.

And Captain Simon and Princess Marie-Rose lived a long and peaceful life. Well, as peaceful as you can get, on the wicked high seas.

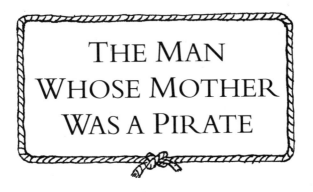

THE MAN WHOSE MOTHER WAS A PIRATE

Margaret Mahy

There was once a little man who had never seen the sea, although his mother was an old pirate woman. The two of them lived in a great city far, far from the seashore.

The little man always wore a respectable brown suit and respectable brown shoes. He worked in a neat office, and wrote down rows of figures in books, ruling lines under them.

Well, one day his mother said, "Shipmate, I want to see the sea again. I want to fire my old silver pistol, and see the waves jump with surprise."

"Oh, Mother!" said the little man. "We haven't got a car, or a bicycle, or a horse. And we've no money, either. All we have is a wheelbarrow and a kite."

"We must make do!" his mother answered sharply. "I will go and load my pistol and polish my cutlass."

The little man went to work.

"Please, Mr. Fat," he begged his boss, "please may I have two weeks' holiday to take my mother to the seaside?"

"I don't go to the seaside!" said Mr. Fat crossly. "Why should you?"

"It is for my mother," the little man explained. "She used to be a pirate."

"Oh, well, that's different," said Mr. Fat who rather wished he were a pirate himself. "But make sure you are back in two weeks, or I will buy a computer."

So off they set, the little man pushing his mother in the wheelbarrow, and his mother holding the kite. His mother wore a green scarf and gold earrings. Between her lips was her old black pipe, behind one ear a crimson rose. The little man wore his brown suit buttoned, and his brown shoes tied. He trotted along pushing the wheelbarrow.

As they went, his mother talked about the sea. She told him of its voices.

"It sings with a booming voice and smiles as it slaps the ships. It screams or sadly sighs. There are many voices in the sea and a lot of gossip, too. Where are the great whales sailing? Is the ice moving in Hudson Bay? What is the weather in Tierra del Fuego? The sea knows the answers to a lot of questions, and one wave tells another."

"Oh yes, Mother," said the little man whose shoes hurt him rather.

"Where are you off to?" asked a farmer.

"I'm taking my mother to the seaside," said the little man.

"I wouldn't go there myself," said the farmer. "It's up and down with the waves, in and out with the tide. The sea doesn't stay put the way a good hill does."

"My mother likes things that don't stay put," said the little man.

Something began to sing in the back of his

mind. "Could that be the song of the sea?" he wondered, as he pushed the wheelbarrow. His mother rested her chin on her knees.

"Yes, it's blue in the sunshine," she said, "and it's gray in the rain. I've seen it golden with sunlight, silver with moonlight, and black as ink at night. It's never the same twice."

They came to a river. There was no boat. The little man tied the wheelbarrow to the kite. A wind blew by, ruffling his collar, teasing his neat mustache.

"Hold tight, Mother!" he called.

Up in the air they went as the wind took the kite. The little man dangled from the kite string. His mother swung in her wheelbarrow-basket.

"This is all very well, Sam," she shouted to him. "But the sea—ah, the sea! It tosses you up and pulls you down. It speeds you along, it holds you still. It storms you and calms you. There's a bit of everything in the sea."

"Yes, Mother," the little man said. The singing in the back of his mind was growing louder and louder. As he dangled from the kite string the white wings of the birds in the sky began to look like the white wings of ships at sea.

The kite let them down gently on the other side of the river.

"Where are you going?" asked a philosopher fellow who sat reading under a tree.

"I'm taking my mother to the sea," said the little man.

"What misery!" cried the philosopher.

"Well, I didn't much like the idea to start with," said the little man, "but now there's this song in the back of my mind. I'm beginning to think I might like the sea when I get there."

"Go back, go back, little man," cried the philosopher. "The wonderful things are never as wonderful as you hope they'll be. The sea is less warm, the joke less funny, the taste is never as good as the smell."

"Hurry up! The sea is calling," shouted the pirate mother, waving her cutlass from the wheelbarrow.

The little man trundled his mother away, and as he ran he noticed that his brown suit had lost all its buttons.

Then something new came into the wind's scent.

"Glory! Glory! There's the salt!" cried his mother triumphantly.

Suddenly they came over the hill.

Suddenly there was the sea.

The little man could only stare. He hadn't dreamed of the BIGNESS of the sea. He hadn't dreamed of the blueness of it. He hadn't thought it would roll like kettledrums, and swish itself on to the beach. He opened his mouth, and the drift and the dream of it, the weave and the wave of it, the fume and the foam of it never left him again. At his feet the sea stroked the sand with soft little paws. Further out, the great, graceful breakers moved like kings into court, tailing the peacock-patterned sea behind them.

The little man and his pirate mother danced hippy-hoppy-happy hornpipes up and down the beach. The little man's clothes blew about in the wind, delighted to be free at last.

A rosy sea captain stopped to watch them.

"Well, here are two likely people," he cried. "Will you be my boatswain, Madam? And you, little man, you can be my cabin boy."

"Thank you!" said the little man.

"Say, 'Aye, aye, sir!' " roared the captain.

"Aye, aye, sir!" replied the little man just as smartly as if he'd been saying "Aye, aye, sir!" all his life.

So Sailor Sam went on board with his pirate mother and the sea captain, and a year later someone brought Mr. Fat a green glass bottle with a letter in it.

"Having a wonderful time," the letter read. "Why don't you run off to sea, too?"

And if you want any more moral to the story than this, you must go to sea to find it.

Acknowledgments

The publisher would like to thank the copyright holders for permission to reproduce the following copyright material:

Joan Aiken: Brandt & Brandt Literary Agents, Inc. for "The Parrot Pirate Princess" from *All and More* by Joan Aiken, Jonathan Cape Ltd. 1971. Copyright © 1971 Joan Aiken. **Ruth Ainsworth**: William Heinemann (a division of Egmont Children's Books Ltd.) for "The Pirate Ship" from *The Pirate Ship and Other Stories* by Ruth Ainsworth, William Heinemann 1980. Copyright © 1980 Ruth Ainsworth. **J.M. Barrie**: Ladybird Books Ltd. for *Peter Pan* by Sir J.M. Barrie retold by Joan Collins, Ladybird Classics 1994. Copyright © 1994 Ladybird Books Ltd. **Sara Conkey**: Scholastic Ltd. for "The Tale of the Bad Ship Torment" from *Story of the Year 2*, Scholastic Ltd. 1994. Copyright © 1994 Sara Conkey. **Geoffrey Hayes**: Random House Inc. for *The Mystery of the Pirate Ghost* by Geoffrey Hayes, Step Into Reading Series, Random House Inc. 1985. Copyright © 1985 Geoffrey Hayes. **Pat Hutchins**: Greenwillow Books (a division of William Morrow & Company, Inc.) for *One-Eyed Jake* by Pat Hutchins, Greenwillow Books, 1979. Copyright © 1979 Pat Hutchins. **Emily Arnold McCully**: Harriet Wasserman Literary Agency, Inc. for *The Pirate Queen* by Emily Arnold McCully, G.P. Putnam & Sons 1995. Copyright © 1995 Emily Arnold McCully. **Colin McNaughton**: Walker Books Ltd., London for *The Pirats: The Amazing Adventures of Anton B. Stanton* by Colin McNaughton, Ernest Benn Ltd. 1979. Copyright © 1979 Colin McNaughton. **Margaret Mahy**: The Orion Publishing Group Ltd. for "The Man Whose Mother Was a Pirate" from *A Lion in the Meadow and Five Other Favorites* by Margaret Mahy, J.M. Dent & Sons Ltd. 1985. Copyright © 1972, 1985 Margaret Mahy. **Arthur Ransome**: Random House U.K. Ltd. for "The Battle in Houseboat Bay" from *Swallows and Amazons* by Arthur Ransome, Jonathan Cape Ltd. 1930. Copyright © 1930 Arthur Ransome. **Tony Robinson**: London Management for "Skulduggery" by Tony Robinson from *Silver Jackanory*, BBC Books 1991. Copyright © 1991 Tony Robinson. **Jon Scieszka**: Penguin U.S.A. Inc. for "Hickory dickory dock" from *The Not-So-Jolly Roger* by Jon Scieszka, The Time Warp Series, Viking 1991. Copyright © 1991 Jon Scieszka. **Robert Louis Stevenson**: Ladybird Books Ltd. for *Treasure Island* by Robert Louis Stevenson, retold by Joyce Faraday, Ladybird Classics 1994. Copyright © 1994 Ladybird Books Ltd.

Every effort has been made to obtain permission to reproduce copyright material, but there may be cases where we have been unable to trace a copyright holder. The publisher will be happy to correct any omissions in future printings.

Titles in the
Kingfisher Treasury series

~

ANIMAL STORIES

BALLET STORIES

BEDTIME STORIES

FIVE-MINUTE STORIES

FUNNY STORIES

GIANT AND MONSTER STORIES

PET STORIES

PIRATE STORIES

PONY STORIES

PRINCESS STORIES

SPOOKY STORIES

STORIES FOR FOUR YEAR OLDS

STORIES FOR FIVE YEAR OLDS

STORIES FOR SIX YEAR OLDS

STORIES FOR SEVEN YEAR OLDS

STORIES FOR EIGHT YEAR OLDS